Cinderella
Sims

Cinderella Sims

Lawrence Block

Subterranean Press • 2003

FIRST EDITION

ISBN
1-931081-51-4

Subterranean Press
P.O. Box 190106
Burton, MI 48519

email:
subpress@earthlink.net

website:
www.subterraneanpress.com

Introduction
by Ed Gorman

Lawrence Block (1938-) writes the best sentences in the business, that business being crime fiction. No tortured self-conscious arty stuff, either. Just pure, graceful, skilled writing of a very high order.

No matter what he writes — the dark Scudder private-eye novels; the spunky Bernie Rhodenbarrs about the kind of thief even a mom could love; or his latest creation, John Keller the hitman, an existential figure full of quirks and kindnesses rare in his profession — no matter what he's telling us, he always makes it sweet to read. He's just so damned nimble and graceful and acute with his language.

By now, his story is pretty well known. Wrote a lot of erotica in the late fifties and early sixties, all the while writing his early crime paperback originals and stories for magazines of every kind. Started becoming a name in crime fiction in the seventies, really broke out in the nineties and is now posed, one would think, for superstardom.

Block has always reminded me of a very intelligent fighter. He knows what he's good at and sticks to his own fight, unmoved by popular fads and critical fancies. He writes about women as well as any male writer I've every read (though since I'm a guy, I may just be saying that he perceives women the same way I do) and he deals with subjects as Oprah-ready as alcoholism and failed fatherhood realistically, yet without resorting to weepiness.

One senses in him sometimes a frustrated mainstream writer. He's always pushing against the restrictions of form and yet never failing to give the reader what he came for in the first place. No easy trick, believe me.

For some reason, I've always hated the word "wordsmith" (probably because it's popular among pretentious young advertising copywriters who don't want to admit that they're writing hymns to beer and dish soap), but that's what Block is. A singer of songs, a teller of tales, a bedazzler.

I read three of his erotic novels and I'll tell you something. They're better written (and we're talking 1958-1961) than half the contemporary novels I read today. He was pushing against form even back then, creating real people and real problems, and doing so in a simple powerful voice that stays with you a hell of a long time.

I wrote the above as a way of setting up a Larry Block novelette I was reprinting in an anthology of pulp stories. I don't see any reason to change a word. Not because they're such graceful or pithy words but because they convey my feelings about Lawrence Block the writer.

I always say that I'm glad to see writers make it up from the trenches and into the sunshine of national prominence. Few writers spent so long in the trenches. Larry sold his first story in 1958. He first hit big in the middle 1990s. That's a long time to breathe the dusty, sometimes dank air of literary obscurity.

Larry began his career, as most of us know by now, selling short stories to the crime magazines of the time and to the sort of paperbacks that local religious groups were always trying to drive from the newsstands.

Introduction

We called these, as I recall, the motley crew of outcasts I hung with in my early college years, right-handers. Suggesting that this type of book inspired one to a certain kind of action few other books did. Except maybe for *Peyton Place* and its imitators. The underlined passages.

I read a lot of Midwood and Beacon and Nightstand novels in those days. I quickly came to realize that some of the writers were much better than others. Max Collier, for example, wrote some of the most perverse books I've ever read. As I remember them, he frequently paired up his bitter hunchbacked heroes with heiresses. Clyde Allison was usually thin on plot but great with patter. Orrie Hitt sometimes got too perverse for my tastes but usually supplied a kind of second-rate James T. Farrell-like blue collar take on the standard "sexy" plots.

And when I say "sexy" I mean "sexy" in the way of the movie comedies of the 1950s and early 1960s. Short on actual details but long on suggestion. And metaphor. Orgasms were frequently portrayed as "searing volcanoes" or some such.

A few of the right-handers were written reasonably well. No great masterpieces slipped through, you understand, but some of the books were actually…kinda sorta actual *novels* rather than just the usual monthly tease.

Which brings us to some guy named Andrew Shaw.

This was one of Larry Block's pen-name circa 1959-1961. Other writers would share the name later on (someday somebody will do an article on how contracts to one writer secretly get handed off by that writer to another writer, a particular form of "ghosting" that goes on at the lower levels of publishing even today) but the early Shaws, at least those I've read, read like Larry Block.

Not the Larry Block of today. The Shaw prose isn't especially polished; the Shaw stories don't always escape cliché; and the Shaw attitude is not unlike the hardboiled crime fiction magazines of the day — i.e., too tough for its own good.

And yet.

Ed Gorman

Yet you can can see in glimpses — and sometimes sustained for long stretches — the Larry Block of today. The idiosyncratic take on modern morality; the dour irony that hides fear and loneliness; and the seeds — just planted — of the style that would become the best of his generation.

Cinderella Sims was originally called *$20 Lust*. The editor obviously spent a long time coming up with that one.

I'm not sure what else Larry was writing at that time. I suspect he was upgrading for an assault on Gold Medal and better-paying markets. I say this because *Cinderella Sims* seems to fall between his sexy books and his early Gold Medal books. Not quite worthy of that little gold medallion but damned close.

One thing Larry Block always had was the ability to move a story forward while giving you detailed character sketches. He has a fast eye for the unusual, the quirks in us, and he makes us come alive with these details. That skill is already apparent in the novel you're holding.

So is his skill in giving you journalistic snapshots of urban American. Re-reading *Cinderella Sims* today is like traveling back in time to that pre-hippie sixties when crew cuts were still the style on college campuses and free love was something only the ridiculous Hugh Hefner experienced.

I'm not going to tell you that this is a great book because it isn't. But it's a damned interesting look at the artist-in-making. I think you'll agree with me that, from the very beginning of his career, Larry Block was a vital and powerful storyteller.

1

I woke up after nine hours of solid sleep and felt like crawling back under the covers again. My mouth had a nauseous taste to it and my head ached in a most peculiar manner, as though the top of it was about ready to fly off and sail across the room. I felt hung over, and this was out of the question if only because I hadn't had more than one or two drinks a day in…well, three months, at the very least. A cold glass of beer at Green's over on Columbus Avenue once an afternoon, that was my limit.

And every afternoon I felt hung over.

While the shower down the hall was turning me from one of the living undead to one of the living dead again, I thought about the way every morning was another morning after, the way every afternoon was a gentle trip to Limbo with a bearded and gaunt Charon at the helm, too tired to pull on the oars. I thought about three months in New York, three months that were supposed to be therapy and that didn't seem to be having much in the way of therapeutic value.

I got out of the shower, tried to get dry with the little postage stamp Mrs. Murdock jokingly called a towel, and finally gave up and padded back to my room. The window was open and the breeze that came through it was as warm as a willing wench. I let it do the job that the towel couldn't do.

Lawrence Block

Therapy. It was half joke and half serious and I never knew just which end was up. If it was doing me any good I couldn't quite see it. But it was better than going back. Bad as it was, it was one hell of a lot better than going back.

Back to a reporter's desk on the *Louisville Times.* Back to a house on Crescent Drive, a small postwar house that was falling apart a little because they never did learn how to build houses after the war was over. A house that was not only falling apart but that was also quite empty; so empty that you could not only hear a pin drop but the fallen pin would echo hysterically in every room.

A cheap, crumbly house. But a house where every room smelled of Mona. Her scent was everywhere, and whether I actually smelled her or only imagined it didn't make much difference at all. She was gone, gone forever, and the little frame house on Crescent Drive still reeked so strongly of her that I would wake up nights with a scream dying on my lips and cold sweat standing up on my forehead.

Those were bad days. I lasted almost two months in Louisville from the day Mona left me. But they were two very bad months. I lived on liquor and prowled dark streets from dusk to dawn, afraid of the house that was empty now, afraid of the night that covered up the city, afraid most of all of myself. Mona Lindsay was gone, gone with a nameless and faceless man, and Ted Lindsay walked empty streets with liquor in his belly and terror in his eyes.

I managed the job. It was easy work by then; after three years swinging Police Beat you can do it with your eyes closed, or half-open at best. There were no murders, no colorful outbreaks of juvenile jollity, nothing that required the services of a sober and serious reporter. All I had to do was drop on down to the station once a night, take the more significant details off the blotter, pound out fifty inches of tripe for the first edition and go back home to sleep.

I did my job and nothing more. The penetrating features, the exciting style, the little insights that had qualified me for

Police Beat to begin with — those weren't there any more. But I swung my desk competently and nobody was going to fire me. Hanovan occasionally told me that my copy was dull, but Hanovan was always telling somebody that unless you turned out Pulitzer-grade copy every time a cat got caught in a tree. I did my job, earned my salary, and lived alone in my own private section of hell.

And I remembered. I remembered Mona — long golden hair breaking over creamy shoulders. Eyes like blue ice, cold and hot at once, ice and fire. I remembered all the delicious details of her delicious body. It was worth remembering — big, firm breasts, beautiful legs, skin as soft as feathers.

So much to remember. How much happens in two years of marriage? How many times had we made love? How many times had I kissed her, touched her, run my hands over that soft smooth skin?

Too many times. Too many times to just throw in the towel and forget it when some smooth-talking son of a bitch picked her up and carried her off into the night.

Too many times.

I would drink without tasting the liquor while it made its way down my throat. Then I would walk all over Louisville and the whole little drama would make its way through my mind. I would try to figure out why it had happened, why it had turned out the way it did. I never did figure it. I'm sure I never will. It happened. Period.

One day they found me sitting on a bench in the park across from a water fountain. I wasn't sleeping, wasn't passed out. I was just sitting with my hands folded neatly in my lap and my eyes focused on nothing special. They talked to me and I didn't answer. Then they stood me up and led me away and showed me to a doctor.

Dr. Strom was all right. A decent guy. For about an hour we just sat staring at each other; then I started talking. I don't remember what I told him and I do not want to remember, but I probably told him damn near everything. He sat through the whole bit without saying a word, just looking at me and nodding now and then.

Then he told me what the therapy would be.

"Lindsay," he said, "I could have you come in three times a week to stretch out on the couch and bitch to me for fifty minutes at a time. You don't want that. I don't want it either. Frankly, I don't think it would do you a hell of a lot of good. You've got something on your mind and you're not going to get rid of it like that."

I agreed with him. I'd considered analysis—I guess everybody does when he runs up against something that turns out to be a little too big for him. But it never appealed to me.

"I'd like you to try something else," he went on. "A rather drastic treatment, perhaps, but one with a much better chance of success."

I waited for him to go on.

"Your life is empty right now," he said. "For the past two years you've been living a certain type of life. In that life your wife has played a predominant role. Now you're attempting to continue living the same life with your wife left out of it. Obviously the life is not going to be a full one. Obviously any life you lead in Louisville now, living in the house where you both lived and seeing the people you both knew — well, such a life is going to be a strain upon you. A tremendous strain."

"What do you suggest?"

"You ought to get out of town," Strom said. "Sell your house, quit your job, head for another town. Take a job that doesn't mean anything to you; something very different from newspaper work. Manual labor or office work or selling, something like that. Go to a big city and let yourself get lost in it. Make new friends, see new people, be alone with yourself. Develop a completely new routine. Read new books. See new movies. Try to find yourself."

I interrupted him. "Look," I said. "Look, it sounds fine. But I can't do that. I've spent one hell of a long time getting where

I am right now. It's my whole life, damn it. I can't just pack up and turn into somebody else. I can't do that. I'd go nuts."

"Nuts?"

I looked at him.

"Nuts?" he repeated. "Lindsay, I wonder if you know just where you are right now. Do you?"

I shook my head.

"You're about three steps away from catatonia," he said. "Schizophrenic catatonia. Keep on the way you're going and one of these days you'll start staring at a wall and you won't stop. I'm not saying this to scare you, but I wouldn't be playing it straight with you if I didn't let you know just how rocky your present situation is. Your present existence is a whirlpool and you're trying to swim out of it. Did you ever hear of anybody swimming out of a whirlpool?"

I found a few more objections and Strom found a few more answers for them. It was no contest—he knew what he was talking about and I didn't, and the more we talked the more I started to realize it. When I left his office I headed for the Times Building, found Hanovan and told him I was leaving. He didn't seem surprised; Strom must have filled him in. He told me he'd have a job for me any time, shook my hand, and left me alone while I cleaned out my desk.

Then I found a relatively trustworthy real estate agent named Greg Cabot, listed my house with him, signed a bunch of papers without reading them, and went back to the house.

Inside it, I smelled her again. It made things just that much more difficult.

I packed a suitcase. I took along some clothes, a toothbrush, and nothing much else. The suitcase was a small one to begin with and I still couldn't manage to fill it up.

So I took her picture along. It was the wrong thing to do, and I realized as I packed it that it was the wrong thing to do, but I couldn't seem to help myself. I packed it, locked the suitcase, heaved it into the backseat of my car and drove to the railroad station where I checked the suitcase in a locker.

Then I drove to the nearest used car lot and sold them my car. It broke my heart to do it but I forced myself. I liked that car. It wasn't much according to the Madison Avenue tastemakers — just a Plymouth convertible five years old with the paint job starting to go. But it was made when they were still trying to make cars that would last instead of playing idiotic games with horsepower and tailfins. The upholstery was good imitation leather and the pickup was impressive. I loved that car. Mona had liked it too — liked to ride in it with the top down and the wind tossing her long yellow hair to hell and gone.

The dealer gave me a lousy two-fifty for it.

I hiked back to the station, reclaimed my suitcase and caught the next train for New York. The train took a long time getting there, stopping at various whistle stops to pick up the milk and get rid of the mail. I chain-smoked, ate a half-million tasteless ham-and-swiss sandwiches, and remembered things that Dr. Strom had told me to forget.

When the train shuddered to a stop in Penn Station I took a temporary room in a cheap hotel in the Times Square area and unpacked. While I was putting my clothes in the dresser with the cockroaches I found the picture of Mona. I stared at it for an hour, maybe longer.

It all came back, of course. Dr. Strom would have bawled hell out of me for it and he would have been right, but Dr. Strom was many hundred miles away and I didn't have him to straighten me out. All I had was the hotel room with its four cold walls, the bed with squeaking springs that reminded me of a motel room where Mona and I had made the walls ring with bed-squeaking. And, of course, I had the picture of Mona. My Mona.

God knows how or when the rift started. My work demanded enough of my time and interest so that I probably never saw the gap begin. Then, when it started widening, I found other things to worry about. I attributed the tension to a batch of convenient scapegoats—job pressure, end of a two-year honeymoon, Mona's desire for a child and our inability thus far to conceive one. More and more often we were staying on our own sides of the big double bed, talking less to each other and, evidently, loving each other less.

Then one night I came home to her and she was packing a suitcase. I looked at her, unable to think of anything clever to say, and she told me quite calmly that she was leaving me.

I don't remember what I said.

She told me his name, which I have since forgotten, although it turned up in the newspaper articles later. The Times didn't carry the story out of some obscure loyalty to me but the Courier plastered it all over page one. But that part comes later.

She was in our bedroom, stuffing the last piece of clothing into her little suitcase and fastening the lid. The big double bed was all neatly made and the unfunny hilarity of that fact struck me—it was just like Mona to make the bed carefully even though she never intended to sleep in it again. She was a meticulous housekeeper, a better-than-average cook, a tigress in bed with the lights out.

Now she was leaving me.

She was saying something but I wasn't listening any more. I was looking at her. I can still remember how she was dressed—stockings and high heels, a very plain brown skirt the color of good chocolate, a canary yellow sweater that buttoned up the back. Her hair was falling free and it looked longer and yellower than ever.

She was a big woman. I'm somewhat better than six feet tall and when she wore heels her nose was level with my mouth. And she had the shape to take care of her height.

She went on talking but I still wasn't listening.

I grabbed her. She tried to twist away from me but I didn't let go of her. I wasn't thinking any more, just acting in a combination of instinct and self-preservation.

I slapped her and she loosened up. I ripped her sweater and all those buttons popped down the back of it like a row of dud firecrackers. I broke the catch on the chocolate brown skirt and tore it off of her. I got rid of the bra and panties. I let her keep the stockings because they didn't get in my way.

I shoved her right down on top of that perfectly made bed and got my own clothes off and tumbled on top of her. She wasn't struggling any more. I think that stopped the minute I ripped her sweater. She was just lying on her back with no expression whatsoever on her beautiful face, lying prone like a sack of flour, a broken doll, a corpse.

I raped her. Coldly and furiously, quickly and savagely. It was not good for me and, of course, it was not at all good for her. It had a beginning and a middle and an ending and then all at once it was over and I had a sickening taste in my mouth.

I rolled away from her, unable to look at her, unable to think about anything at all. I tried to stand up but I didn't make it and I had to sit back down on the bed again. She stood up and began dressing once again. She put on fresh clothes and put the ones I had torn off back into her suitcase. For a long time she didn't say anything.

Then she said: "I hope you enjoyed yourself, Ted."

I told her I was sorry. I meant it, too, but somehow it came out sounding sarcastic.

"I'm still leaving, Ted. You can't stop me."

And of course she was right. I couldn't stop her, and so I didn't try. I let her go and when she was gone I began to cry. I hadn't cried in years but I cried now. It hurt.

I think I got drunk that night. It's hard to remember now but that's probably what I did. And I'm positive I cried some more, and shook, and swore an oath that I would find her and get her back where she belonged if it killed me.

That turned out to be impossible.

A car from the Sheriff's Office found them the next day. The nameless, faceless bastard who took her away had one of those cute little foreign jobs, a sports model that could take

18

hairpin curves at eighty, only either the car goofed or the name-less, faceless bastard wasn't much of a driver. At any rate the cute little foreign job missed one of those hairpin curves and did an end-over-end off the side of a convenient cliff.

There was hardly enough left to bury.

And so my wife had left me, and all the oaths in the world would not reclaim her. She was gone, quite irretrievably gone, and there was certainly no way of getting her back.

This time I didn't cry. This time I simply drank.

So I looked at the picture which I shouldn't have lugged to New York to begin with, looked at it long and hard for perhaps an hour and thought all the thoughts that Dr. Strom would have disapproved of so violently. After the hour or so had passed I took the picture, kissed it somewhat melodramatically, tore it into a thousand little celluloid threads and flushed them down the ancient toilet in the bathroom down the hall.

I went to sleep and dreamed bad dreams.

After a few days in the hotel I got a room and a job in that order. Neither was much to write home about, but for that matter there was nobody at home to write to. The room guaranteed that I wouldn't die of exposure; the job guaranteed that I wouldn't die of starvation. What more can anybody ask?

The room was in an old brownstone on West 73rd Street between Columbus and Amsterdam. It was a fourth-floor walkup, a little room with a single bed, a scarred dresser and a chair that might have qualified as an antique if it hadn't been so ugly and broken down. There was a bathroom down the hall where the cockroaches could lead me every morning. The room cost ten dollars a week, which was reasonable, and the landlady was a sad-looking old baby who let me know that I could drink as much as I wanted as long as I didn't puke, and screw as much as I wanted as long as I didn't break the bed. It seemed decent enough.

The job came after the room, because I wanted to find something I could walk to rather than fight the IRT every morning and evening. I passed up the HELP WANTED: MALE section of the Times and wandered around the area looking for a job that didn't require much in the way of talent.

It was an interesting neighborhood to wander around. There were a large number of faggots and dykes, the more subdued ones who thought it was gauche to live in the Village, a batch of Irish who drank in the wonderful bars on Columbus Avenue, a scattering of Puerto Ricans, and throughout a sprinkling of various Manhattan types. The neighborhood was small stores and bars and shops on Columbus and Amsterdam, bigger stores and restaurants on 72nd Street, and mostly brownstones with an occasional brick building on the side streets. Here and there you could find a tree, if you cared about it. I didn't.

Central Park was just a block and a half away, which was nice if you cared about birds and grass and flowers and fresh air. Again, I didn't.

There was a *Help Wanted* card in a window on Columbus and I took a long look at the place that wanted help. It looked as though they could use it. A big weather-beaten sign said the place was Grace's Lunch and advised the world to drink Coca-Cola. The window needed a scrubbing and so, by the looks of things, did the people who ate there.

I went inside. There were half a dozen tables with chairs around them and maybe twice as many stools at the counter. A battered dame in her thirties with frizzy black hair was dividing her time between the counter and the cash register. There seemed to be somebody in the back cooking up the slop for her to serve. About eight or ten customers were shoveling it down.

I pulled up a stool and the dame with the hair came over and shoved a menu at me. It was dog-eared around the edges and contained a lot of food. Somebody's fried eggs were stuck to it in one spot; the rest I couldn't identify.

I gave the menu back to her. "I ate a little while ago," I told her. "I'm looking for a job."

"Ever sling hash before?"

"Sure," I lied.

"Nothing much to it, actually. No cooking — Carl takes care of that end. Just take the orders, pour the coffee and like that. We don't get much of a rush here. Just neighborhood people who know the place, regulars that come in all the time. You look at this place from the front and it doesn't make much of a show. The grub's good and the regulars know it. They don't care how fancy it is."

I filled in with a nod.

"My name's Grace," she told me. "I own the place. I need somebody nights from midnight to eight. Horrible hours for most people. It gets tough to keep help those hours. A guy'll take the job, then quit me cold in a week or two as soon as his belly's full. If you're going to pull that bit I don't need you. If you want to be steady the work's here for you. The job pays forty a week and meals. You get to stuff yourself as much as you want while you work only don't eat up all the profits or I'll fire you. Try to cheat me and I'll catch you. Sound fair enough to you?"

"Fair enough. I'm just looking for steady work."

"That's what it is. You don't mind the hours?"

I was used to them. I told her I didn't mind at all. And the job turned out to be simple enough. Grace couldn't have gotten rich on the midnight-to-eight shift; the bulk of the trade was coffee-an' with an occasional ham and eggs thrown in. Most of the time the place was half empty; sometimes Carl and I would talk to each other without seeing a single customer for twenty minutes at a clip.

But the food was good and the pay was enough to live on. I spent April and May settling down into a strange sort of routine, the general type of life that Dr. Strom had said would do me the most good. Up at four or five in the afternoon, coffee on a hot plate in my room, a magazine in my room or a movie around the corner on Broadway. A walk, a nap or something until it was time to go to work.

Then eight hours of work, broken up with a meal or two and a few rounds of the harmless and generally useless conversation a counterman has with a customer. I got to know the regulars — a couple of cabbies who made a stop at Grace's once or twice a night for coffee, a bartender from Maloney's who'd stop in for a bite as soon as his place was closed for the night, a waitress who ended her shift at four and a batch of guys and dolls whom I knew only by their faces.

It was supposed to be therapy. I was completely alone, as alone as a person could be who still talked to people, still breathed city air and still walked in city streets. No one knew more about me than my name. No one asked where I was from, what I was doing, where I was headed. Come to think of it, Grace was the only person in New York outside of my landlady who knew my last name. To everybody else I was Ted, or Hey, You.

I think I understand what Strom had in mind. Bit by bit every shred of the identity of Ted Lindsay, Reporter, was evaporating. At first I would glance through the New York papers with the eye of a pro, but now all I read were the stories themselves. Fine points flew by me; I was too immersed in other things to bother with them. They didn't matter at all any more.

And, as Ted Lindsay disappeared, Mona Lindsay gradually faded into the background. As I lost consciousness of myself the woman who was lost forever gradually ebbed into oblivion, or Limbo, or whatever is the abode of lost and forgotten souls. This isn't to say that I forgot her, because forgetting Mona would have been like forgetting a white cow. You know the bit? Try not to think of a white cow. See what I mean?

But I would test myself now and then, trying to think of her without caring, trying to remember her without getting a hard painful spot in my chest about where your heart is supposed to be. It got progressively easier. Away from Louisville, away from the Times Building, away from our home and our friends and all the places where we had been together, the memories of her were far less compelling, far less vivid and real.

It should have been ideal. By all rules it should have been ideal, just an inch or two short of Nirvana. It wasn't, and this was a constant source of irritation to me. It didn't send me screaming, didn't drive me to drink in the cool green Irish bars on Columbus Avenue, for the elementary reason that there was nothing to scream about, nothing to drink over.

There was no pain.

But pleasure is more than the absence of pain. And, all in all, the life I was leading was totally devoid of pleasure. One day followed the next with mechanical precision. Eight hours of nothing was followed by eight hours of work which in turn was followed by eight hours of sleep. Life was three shifts of eight hours each, seven of these groups of three making a week. The worst day in each week was Sunday — then I had to find something to do to fill in the eight hours when I would otherwise have been working.

The monotony of it was occasionally overpowering. Little things became very important — taking my shirts to the laundry was a big thing, even if Toy Lee didn't have much to say to me when I handed him my shirts or picked them up. A haircut was a big deal. I never bought much of anything, but I window-shopped constantly, furnishing an apartment mentally and buying a whole new wardrobe in my mind.

It wasn't enough.

There were needs, basic and human needs. The need for a woman, of course. I hadn't had a woman since Mona left. I suppose there were opportunities for that — lonely women nursing cups of lukewarm coffee at the lunch counter, whores walking up and down Broadway, that sort of thing. But I hardly knew where to begin.

I was out of practice. Two years of marriage plus a year of courtship added up to three years without another woman than Mona. The role of wolf was a foreign one; I would have felt ridiculous approaching a girl.

The need for someone to talk to was even more important, actually. Living alone, eating alone, never talking about anything more far-reaching than the weather or the murders in the tabloids—this didn't make for the world's most stimulating existence. I didn't know anybody, didn't get any letters or write any.

But no single need seemed to be important enough for me to do anything about it. If I had needed a woman badly enough, I suppose I would have found one who would have been obliging. If I had needed a friend badly enough, it's logical to guess that I would have found one over the counter at Grace's or over a beer at Green's. I read somewhere that a man gets anything in the world if he wants it badly enough. But I couldn't even want anything, not deeply enough for it to matter inside, where it counted.

So it was mid-June, and I dried myself with warm air from the window and boiled water in the teakettle on the hot plate. The water boiled and the kettle whistled. I spooned instant coffee into a white china cup and poured water on it. I stirred it with a spoon, set it on the sill to cool and looked out across the courtyard at somebody's washing. When the coffee was cool I drank it, then washed out the cup in the bathroom and put it away.

I walked down three flights of stairs as usual, stole a look at the heap of mail as usual—which was silly, since no one on Earth knew my address—and, as usual, walked out of the building and down the steps.

Outside, a damned fine day was finishing up. There's a line in a song that goes *I like New York in June. How about you?* and it makes good sense. New York is eminently likable in June with the air warm and the skies generally clear. Later in the summer it gets too hot, far too hot, but in June it's better than any other time. The sky was clear as good gin and the air even smelled clean. I took deep breaths of it and felt good.

I walked around the corner to the candy store and exchanged a dime for a copy of the *Post*. Then I wandered over to the park and found an empty bench to sit on while I made my way through the paper to find out what if anything was new in the world. Nothing much was. Some politicians were trying to decide to cut out nuclear tests without managing to accomplish much of anything, some local crime commissions were investigating some local crime, God was in his heaven and all was wrong with the world.

There were only two stories that I read all the way through. One told about a young mother in Queens who had meticulously removed her husband's genitals with a grapefruit knife; the other reported on a teenager in Flatbush who'd gotten jealous over his girlfriend and then cut off her breasts with a switchblade. I thought that the two of them ought to get together, and then I thought that the *New York Post* ought to be ashamed of itself; and then I thought that maybe I ought to be ashamed of myself. I threw the paper in a trashcan and left the park before dark. Only mad dogs and Englishmen walk in Central Park after the sun goes down.

I bought a bag of peanuts from a sad-looking peanut vendor at the 72nd Street gate. It was an ordinary day, this time an ordinary day with peanuts. I ate the peanuts and threw the shells in the gutter. I kept walking.

I thought about things. Maybe Dr. Strom had either shot his wad or accomplished his mission in life. Maybe it was due time for me to get the hell out of New York and back to Louisville where I belonged. The Police Beat at the *Times* was infinitely more exciting than slinging hash at Grace's Lunch. The house on Crescent Drive was far more livable than the brownstone on 73rd Street. Ted Lindsay, Reporter was a considerably more exciting individual than Ted Lindsay, Nobody.

Perhaps I was cured. Now I could go back to my home and settle down again, take an apartment a few blocks from the Times Building and get my old job back: Hanovan would find work for me, even push some deserving bum out in order to get me back where I belonged. All I had to do was ask him.

Lawrence Block

I thought about this, and I thought about other things, and I thought about how nice it would be to feel alive again.

And then I saw the girl.

2

The impact of the girl defies description. It wasn't just the femaleness of her — she had the effect that anything impossibly striking and beautiful can have upon a person. I suppose a sailor who hasn't seen dry land in years might react the way I did when he catches a glimpse of shoreline. She was all the seven wonders of the world rolled into one, a symphony of beauty, and for several eternal seconds I couldn't breathe or move. I could only look at her and be happy that she was there.

How do you describe something lovely? Summarizing the various components doesn't do the trick; in this case the whole is a great deal more than the sum of its separate parts. I can tell you that her hair was black as sin, that she wore it short and pixieish. I can tell you that her skin was as white as virginity personified, white and clear and pure. She was wearing plaid Bermuda shorts that showed enough of her legs to assure me that her legs were good from top to bottom. She was wearing a charcoal grey sweater that let me know that legs were not her only strong points.

But that doesn't do her justice. It shows that she was pretty; that the various parts of her were in good order. It doesn't show the girl herself, the beauty of her, the radiant quality that reached with both hands across the width of 73rd Street like a

Lawrence Block

human magnet, reached me and grabbed me and would not
let go.

You have to get the picture. I was on the downtown side of
73rd Street on my way back from the 72nd Street entrance to
the park. She was on the uptown side of the street, walking
west the same as I was, going from God-knew-where to God-
knew-where. She was walking fairly quickly. I couldn't walk
because I was too busy looking at her.

Then I was able to walk again. I followed her — not con-
sciously, not purposely, but without even being able to think
about it. She walked and I walked and my eyes must have
burned two small holes in the back of that sweater that so inti-
mately hugged the top half of her body.

She waited for the light at the corner of Columbus. So did
I. But I didn't look at the light. I looked at her, and when she
started across the street I crossed in step with her. My eyes
stayed with her.

Her walk was poetry, her body music, the toss of her head
pure ballet. I found myself hoping she'd go on walking clear
over to the Hudson so that I could go on with her. I think if she
had walked to the edge of the river and had proceeded to hotfoot it across to Jersey I would have followed until I drowned.
For the first time I understood how those rats and mice felt
when they followed the Pied Piper of Hamelin. They simply
couldn't help themselves.

Halfway down the block she stopped, turned and went
down a flight of stairs, disappeared. I would have followed
her if I could but it was fairly obvious that her apartment was
off bounds to me. It didn't seem fair.

For several minutes I stood on my side of the street watching the building she had entered. Evidently she lived in the
basement apartment in that particular brownstone, a building
quite indistinguishable from the identical brownstones on either side of it. I stood there, watching, committing the address
to careful memory. Then it hit me all at once and I realized
where I was.

28

I was standing right in front of my own building.

I couldn't believe it at first. I looked around, very cautiously, and sure enough, that was where I was. I was smack dab in front of Mrs. Murdock's home for wayward newspapermen. The girl of my dreams lived across the street from me, with her bed twenty or forty yards from mine. It seemed impossible.

I told myself that she must have just moved in, that if she had ever been there before I would have known it. Nothing like that could be within a mile of me without my noticing her, sensing her presence.

But who was she? Where had she come from? What was she doing, whoever she was?

I had to know. All the questions — the *who what where when why and how* that are burned so deeply into a reporter's brain — they haunted me now. I had to find out about her.

The first step was simple. It required my getting the hell off the streets before the dog catcher saw me standing with my tongue hanging out and carted me off to the pound. It took a little work but I managed it. I dragged myself back to Columbus and aimed myself at Green's. The notion of a cold glass of beer seemed tremendously appealing all of a sudden. Maybe because I was sweating.

I took a stool and the bartender brought me a glass of beer. He did this without asking. I was a regular at Green's, although hardly the kind of regular that kept them in meat and potatoes. I was in there once a day, rain or shine, and each and every time I nursed one small glass of draft beer for half an hour or so, paid my fifteen cents and left.

There were plenty of the other sort of regulars. They started early at Green's and I knew they would be there until the place closed, drinking their lives away slowly, never getting too drunk and never drawing what could be honestly described as a sober breath. Many times I'd thought about them, about the way they spent their lives, and many times I'd figured out that I would have wound up that way if I hadn't left Louisville.

The bar wouldn't be Green's but it would amount to the same thing. One of the run-down joints on East Cedar Street where old reporters go when they don't get lucky and die of cirrhosis instead.

I sipped my beer. I left the lushes to their alcoholic poison and thought of more intriguing things.

Like the girl.

The hell of it was, she was just what I needed to make my life complete. No sarcasm here—this is the straight dope. Before Little Miss Vision waltzed into my life there was nothing for me—no pleasure, no joy, no imagination, nothing but the monotony of a day-to-day routine that had become increasingly stifling. Now, however, Little Miss Vision had transformed the monotony to fascinating frustration. Now, instead of being bored, I was enhanced, entranced, and ready to be romanced.

Which seemed to be a new version of screwed, glued and tattooed.

Well.

I now had problems—which was, if nothing else, a change from monotony. Problem the first was to find out who in the world the lithe little brunette was. Problem the second was to get to know her. Problem the third, of course, was to get into her pants.

In Louisville the first two problems wouldn't exist. I would simply say hello to her and she would say hello to me and I would take it from there. But New York was hysterically different. In New York you were considered horrifyingly square if you were on a first-name basis with anyone who lived within a one-mile radius of your residence. In New York you could live across the hall from someone for a lifetime without ever saying hello. And, in New York, if you said hello to a pretty girl on a street you were a masher and subject to arrest, conviction, and permanent residence in the Tombs; an unpleasant prospect at best.

I sipped some more beer and, amazingly, the glass was empty.

This gave me pause. It was a warm day and I had built up a fairly substantial thirst. I certainly could have made good use of a second glass of beer. Hell, I would have loved a second glass of beer. But my life was ordered in such a manner that certain habits had become damnably difficult to break.

I paid fifteen cents for the glass I'd just downed and left Green's, still thirsty. It was warmer out, which struck me as somewhat silly in view of the fact that it was after six and time for New York to start cooling off for the night. But there was no doubt about it—it was warmer, and the freshness of the day was getting sponged up by a palling mugginess that had sneaked in from Jersey. The breezes had given up for the evening. It was, suddenly and very annoyingly, damned uncomfortable.

I headed back toward my room, then changed my mind and crossed the street to her side of the block. Already in my mind that side had an identity—it was *her* side as surely as if she had owned every bit of property on it. Before it was just the other side of the block. Now it belonged to her, whoever she might turn out to be.

I stopped in front of her apartment and screwed up my courage for a look at her window. It didn't reveal anything— bamboo curtains obscured any view I might have otherwise had of my newly beloved. I cursed them, but I had to admit they were nice curtains. What the hell.

What next? All sorts of absurdities suggested themselves to me and one was sillier than the next. I could ring her doorbell and pretend I was a lost seaman from Canarsie. I could tell her I was a census taker and ask her some statistical type questions, like what was her name and how old she was and would she like to have dinner with me. Brilliant notions, all of them.

Think, Lindsay. You're supposed to be a reporter. You've got a hot tip that you have to run down — which of course was ridiculous, because reporters only got hot tips in movies. But this is the way I was carrying on about them.

When the notion came to me it was disgustingly simple, the way most good notions are. I went into the brownstone's main entrance — not the basement, but the front foyer — and looked at the row of name plates with doorbells attached. At the bottom of a long list of nameless names I found Apartment B, which obviously meant basement. I looked at the name next to it.

I did not believe it.

There was this black strip of plastic, and in white relief it said, for all the world to see, all bold and brazen in its simplicity, CINDERELLA SIMS.

Sure.

So, sharp reporter that I was, I immediately rejected that one and read through all the other names. Maybe Cinderella Sims was the janitoress and they had a different listing for the basement apartment. Maybe I was in the wrong building. Maybe I had managed to slip into a different space-time continuum or something.

Maybe anything.

I floated out of the vestibule and down the stairs and across the street. Either my mind wasn't functioning properly or something, but I felt a little dizzy and a small voice in the back of my head shouted Cinderella Sims until my eardrums threatened to explode. Implode, that is. Explode is when something bursts open from inside, like an overinflated balloon. Implode is when something bursts inward, like a vacuum bulb. It doesn't make a hell of a lot of difference, but, well, you know.

There was a book in my room that I hadn't finished yet, a novel by Ben Christopher called *A Sound of Distant Drums*. It wasn't the greatest thing since vaudeville but I managed to get lost in it and kill the too many hours before it was time to go to work.

I hauled my chair over to the window, eased myself into it, propped the book open on my lap and rested my feet on the windowsill. Every so often I would look up from the book and gaze out of the window in the hope that Cinderella Sims would treat me to a glimpse of her beautiful body.

A few minutes before twelve I was taking my apron from the hook in back and telling Grace to take off whenever she felt like it. I let Carl know that a mushroom omelet wouldn't be bad, picked up a dishcloth and wiped a few places on the counter that Grace hadn't bothered with. She always seemed to leave some recent dirt around for me to amuse myself with. It was something to do.

The night started slow and promptly died. It was a Wednesday, which is never the most exciting night in the week and was setting out to prove the validity of that statement this particular evening. When I took over from Grace there were two Puerto Rican fellows gulping coffee at the counter and one shopworn old maid polishing off the special one buck minute steak. The old maid took off a few minutes after I came on and the Puerto Ricans had another cup of joe apiece before they vanished. They both left tips, which is rare when all you order is coffee. The old maid more than made up for them by taking up a table, spending a buck and not leaving anything: Such is life.

I ate my mushroom omelet. Carl makes damn good mushroom omelets if you care for mushroom omelets, which I happen to. The joint was happily empty while I ate, permitting me to contemplate why an old maid would be eating a minute steak at such a late hour anyway. Maybe she was just getting up. Hell, she didn't have anything to stay in bed for.

With this observation, a whole new vista opened to me. The Lindsay method of behavior analysis. To hell with Freud. To hell with Jung and Adler. To hell, for that matter, with Strom. The Lindsay Method of Behavior Analysis (I was writing it in mental capital letters now) provided the perfect key to understanding the inner emotions that ruled the lives of ordinary people.

Like this:

A person acts funny if he isn't getting plenty.

There were corrollaries. The funnier a person acted, the less he was getting. If a person acted normal, he either was getting enough or he didn't know what he was missing.

It was ingenious. It was the most fundamental observation since Murphy's Law. It was perfection.

And I was pleased with myself.

I also needed it even more than the old maid. According to the Lindsay method, she didn't know what she was missing. Hell, I knew what I was missing. I was missing Mona, but there was no sense crying over spilled flesh. I was also missing Cinderella Sims, and in addition I was missing all the other succulent female flesh that walked the sensual sinful streets of the sensual sinful city of New York.

Which was annoying.

Two young hoods wandered in. You know the type — they look as though they just stepped out of a 42nd Street B movie, with black leather jackets and ducktail haircuts and stomping boots. The movies probably give them their inspiration, I don't know.

They took seats at the counter and I got uneasy. It always makes me uneasy when juvies come into the place and I'm all alone out there.

So what happened? So they each ordered black coffee; smoked three cigarettes apiece, left half their coffee, put half a buck on the counter for the two cups and told me to keep the change. I don't know — you can take your sweet little old ladies and shove them. Give me the no-good bastards any day of the week.

But this still didn't do much for my sex life.

So I went over to the side to jaw a little with Carl. This wasn't designed to do anything for my sex life either, as Carl and I could hardly have been less interested in each other in that respect. Come to think of it, I don't think sex in any form made a hell of a difference to Carl. All he cared about was cooking and drinking, and not in that order.

He was a bow-legged old goof, half English and half Irish, and years ago he'd shipped all over the world as cook on a variety of leaky freighters. He was one of those guys who always had a three-day growth of beard on his face. I don't know whether it was because his beard didn't grow any longer or because he never changed the blade in his razor. Maybe nobody ever told him you needed a blade in your razor. Whatever it was, beautiful he was not.

But he could cook like a stove. He kept a quart of white port in the kitchen cupboard and swigged it quite openly but Grace worked like a dog to pretend not to notice it. She had this self-imposed rule against keeping an alcoholic on the payroll, and if there was ever an alcoholic, Carl was it. If she let herself admit this little fact she would have been honor-bound to chuck him out on his ear, which would have knocked her business into Kings County. So she ignored the bottle and Carl cooked a blue streak and everybody was happy, especially the customers.

"Carl," I said, "I need a woman."

"Everybody does."

"I mean it," I said. "I need a woman."

"In this neighborhood," he said thoughtfully, "even the women need a woman now and then. You seen the fleet of dykes we been getting lately?"

"Many of them?"

He shook his head as if every incidence of lesbianism was depriving him of a potential conquest. "A pair of 'em came in here this afternoon, one of 'em you couldn't of told from a man. Without you turn her upside-down and have a good look, that is."

I forgot to mention another of Carl's virtues. He worked sixteen hours a day. This can make a hard-headed business woman like Grace overlook one hell of a lot of white port. And why not? Like in the song, a good man is hard to find. Especially at the wages she was handing out.

"These dykes," he was saying. "I got a look at 'em through the serving slot, you know. You took a close look, you could tell the one was a broad underneath it all. Probably even had a pair of boobs on her, although I'll lay odds she was embarrassed that she did. But the other one. A doll. A doll."

"Yeah?" My conversation was a little less than brilliant.

"A redhead," he said. "Not a freckle-face redhead. A peaches-and-cream redhead. Built for action. And I would stand there, you know, and I would think about this dirtpicking dyke and the things she'd be doing to this peaches-and-cream redhead, those hammy hands on the chick and her mouth and everything, and the peaches-and-cream redhead squirming around and loving it and all, and let me tell you, it made me sick to my stomach."

"The redhead was really something, huh?"

He shook his head, his eyes as sad as a Charlie Chaplin movie. "Built," he said. "Built for action. I got a look at her going out when she stood up. Boobs on her out to here. A behind with a motion like a pogo stick. I thought about her and that dyke, you know, and I got an idea what the two of 'em would be doing. It made me sick."

Him it made sick. Me it made more frustrated than ever. I needed that talk with Carl like I needed a broken collarbone.

"They ordered eggs," he said. "Fried and over, you know. Let me tell you, I burned those eggs. I burned 'em crisp as leather. Maybe crisper."

The redhead who came in a few minutes of four was not the peaches-and-cream variety. She was the freckle-faced variety, and if she was a lesbian I was the faggot's Prince of Wales.

No woman ever oozed heterosexual sex the way this one did. No woman since Cleopatra. Possibly no woman since Sheba. Possibly no woman since Eve.

She wasn't pretty. Her nose was too big and her forearms were too fat and her eyes were bloodshot. But her breasts were a pair of warm pineapples and her lips were the color of spilled blood and the look in her eyes said something that rhymes with pluck-me.

She wanted a hamburger and a Coke. I told Carl and he put down the bottle and went to work. Then, because Cinderella Sims had set fire to a fuse which had lain dormant all too long, I went back and leered across the counter at her. She leered right back at me. She seemed even more interested in the leering process than I was, which was saying a lot. My tongue may well have been hanging out. This should give you the general idea.

"You're cute," she said.

"So are you."

"That's not all," she said. "I'm more than cute, I'm good at it."

"At what?"

"At what you're thinking about."

I tried to look innocent. I'm sorry to say that it didn't come off.

"What's your name?"

"Ted."

"Mine's Rosie."

"Hi, Rosie."

"Hi, Ted."

Our dialogue wasn't the best since Tarzan and Jane. Me, I'll take Harpo Marx any time.

"What you looking at me like that for, Ted?"

"I like the way you're put together."

"Yeah?"

I nodded solemnly.

"It's all me."

"Honest?"

"Don't you believe me?"

I shrugged.

"So grab a feel. I won't miss it."

I reached over the counter and took hold of one of her big breasts. The whole thing was coarse and crude and vulgar but the breast in my hand was the first I'd had hold of in months. Too many months.

And it worked for both of us. I got more excited over the whole thing than I care to admit and she was evidently the type of gal with a short fuse. She was ready to go then and there. Her eyes seemed to be swimming in heat and her mouth was open, her upper lip glistened with sweat.

"Ted —"

I let go of her breast. It wasn't something I felt like letting go of too easily.

Carl broke the spell. He rang a little bell and I went back to pick up the burger and draw a glass of Coke for her. He was waiting for me at the window, his eyes wary.

"Teddy boy," he said, "that one you should watch out for. Give her a wide berth. She's poison."

"You know her?"

"Don't have to," he told me. "I know her type. She'll turn you inside out and holler for more. She'll draw you and drain you until your knees won't work any more. She'll have you so tired you won't be able to work for the next month and a half. Watch out, boy."

I grinned at him. "Maybe I need some of that, Carl. It's been a long time."

He sighed. "How long? Ten years? Twenty years? Me, I could go twenty years before I'd want to tangle with one like her. She'll eat you alive, Ted. She'll drink your blood and use your skin for a snot rag. You young fellows, you don't know anything but get on and ride. Me, I'd give her a wide berth."

Young fellows. When I hit thirty I thought people would stop thinking of me as a young fellow. They didn't, somehow.

"I'll see what happens," I told him. "Like I say, it's been a long time."

I brought her her food and traded wisecracks with her for a while. Every look at her and every look from her made me a little more anxious to get next to her, but at the same time Carl's words had had a mildly sobering effect. I wanted to make it with her, but I didn't want to talk about it.

Eddie saved me.

Eddie's a cop who looks as though he couldn't be anything else without looking out of place. He's a heavy-set flatfoot who generally stops by for coffee-an' about that time of night. When he came in I had an excuse to leave Rosie alone and make like a counterman. The excuse seemed to satisfy her. Obviously I couldn't play with her breasts with a cop in the room. It made good sense.

Eddie and I had never had a hell of a lot to say to each other in the past, but this time we did it up brown. I was very clever about the whole thing if I say so myself. I made it seem as though Eddie was leading me and I couldn't cut the conversation short without being obnoxious about it. Actually I was doing the leading, but happily neither Eddie nor my freckle-face tumbled to that end of it.

She left before Eddie did and I was vaguely relieved to see her go. I wanted her—any man would have—but I suppose you could say I was a little bit afraid of her. Carl's message had hit home. She looked like the kind of girl who needed an army, and although that can be a man's dream when he's sort of hard up, I'd met up with a girl like that before. She couldn't get enough, and no matter how much I gave her she was still itching for more. In its own way this can be one hell of a frustrating experience.

When Eddie left I went back and picked up Rosie's tab. It came to forty-five cents and there was a quarter and two dimes on the counter beside it. No tip, and I don't suppose I really had one coming.

Then, when I was carrying the check to the register to ring it up, I saw the penciled scrawl on the back:

Lawrence Block

Your tip's waiting for you at 114 West 69th Street. Apt. 3-C. Ring Twice.

There it was—straight and not at all subtle, right on the line. I rang up the sale, spilled the forty-five cents into the register and spiked the tab. And visions of red hair on a white pillowslip flooded my brain.

And there it was. What could be simpler? All I had to do was hotfoot it over to 114 West 69th as soon as my shift limped to a halt, ring her bell twice, race upstairs and try my luck with the redoubtable Rosie. A half-year's accumulation of sexual inactivity ought to last me a long time, even with an insatiable maiden like Rosie.

The funny thing is, I was resisting the whole notion not because of a fear of what Rosie could do to me, or anything like that, but for an entirely different reason. It was, I realized, out of some perverse loyalty to a girl I had never met, a girl with the improbable name of Cinderella Sims.

Which was ridiculous.

Totally ridiculous.

I closed my eyes and tried to focus the face of Cinderella Sims on my brain. It didn't work. I had seen her once, and for no more than a matter of minutes. I couldn't even picture her face, although of course I would recognize her at once, any time, anywhere.

All that I could remember was that she was the most beautiful girl in the world.

For all I knew she was as gay as the pair of lesbians Carl had described in such unglowing terms. Or she could be married, or frigid, or deaf, or her teeth could be bad and her speech all impedimented and—

Hell. I didn't believe a thought of it. She was perfection, damn it. How often in life do you run up against perfection? How often do you find something that couldn't be improved, not one whit, not one speck, not at all?

Not very often.

So here she was, and here I was, and here Rosie was. Miss Cinderella Sims was temporarily unobtainable but this alone was no call for me to throw myself away on a most imperfect specimen who offered nothing but temporary sexual relief. What the hell—I'd been living in silly celibacy for half a year.

There was no point to throwing it all away on a sexbomb who'd probably given it away to half the male population of the island of Manhattan.

So it's easy to see what I did next. I finished up, you see, and then I went straight home. Straight home to my own little room, where I got undressed, got in bed, pulled up the sheet, blew a kiss to my somnolent beloved and went off to sleep.

And that, of course, is what I did.

Right?

Wrong.

I finished up, all right. Grace took over at eight on the button—she was another idiot who didn't mind a sixteen-hour day—and a monkey named Leon relieved Carl, who took his jug of wine and went home. I hung up my apron, had a wake-up cup of joe and went out into the morning rush hour air, which was horrible.

But I did not go home.

I went elsewhere.

I went to 114 West 69th Street. Up the stairs, into the front vestibule. I looked at the nameplates and found out that Rosie's last name was Ryan.

She was lucky on that score. If it had been O'Grady I would have gotten the hell out of there once and for all. Sweet Rosie O'Grady at eight o'clock in the goddamned morning is a bit much.

Or if she lived on Washington Square. You know the song:
Rose of Washington Square
With all the pomade in your hair
You once were called Roger
But now, you draft-dodger

Lawrence Block

You're Rose of Washington Square.

Well, anyhow. I stood in that vestibule and thought about things, but not too deeply. And then I found the bell for her apartment, Apt. 3-C.

And I rang it.

Twice.

3

The silence was like a woman yawning. Then a buzzer shattered it. I leaned on the door and it opened. I was in the elevator on the way to the fourth floor before the buzzer shut up.

There were four apartments to a floor so I didn't have a hell of a lot of trouble finding 3-C. I hit the bell, ringing twice again for the hell of it, and waited like a college kid at a whorehouse until the door opened.

I caught my breath.

"Come on in," she said. "You had me worried for a while there. I didn't know whether or not you were going to show up. I was all ready for bed and everything, and here you are."

There I was. And there she was all ready for bed and everything. She was barefoot and all she was wearing was this pink silk affair that didn't do a hell of a lot to protect her from the elements. It must have been thrown together during the war when they were short of silk.

I could see her nipples through it.

She had to close the door because I didn't have the strength. I reached for her instantly but she sidestepped, a coy little smile on her coy little face, and suddenly I felt very foolish. I was out of practice. There is a rigid code of play in affairs of this nature and I was a little rusty on the ground rules. Maybe you think it's a cinch to find yourself in a fairly decent apartment with the greatest thing since sex was invented. It's not that simple. You have to be very cool about the whole thing, and I wasn't.

"Easy," she said. "Easy, baby. There's plenty here and it won't spoil. Take your time. Have a seat. Let me fix you a drink."

She pointed to a couch and I sank into it like a grateful refugee from a Chinese prison camp. While she disappeared to concoct drinks I looked around the apartment and wondered how she paid for it. I had a pretty good idea, but what the hell.

"Straight or how?"

"Water," I said. Straight liquor at eight in the morning is fine for some people. So is straight heroin. Me, I'm just a country boy.

She came back with two glasses and gave one of them to me. There was too much bourbon in it and not too much water but I took an obliging sip from it and set the glass down on the leather-top coffee table. I wondered if the glass would make a mark on the table and decided that, all things considered, I didn't give a damn.

She sat down next to me and she was so close I could smell her. There was no water in the glass, just bourbon. She polished off half of it in one swallow.

I reached for her.

"Easy," she said a second time. "You can't expect a girl to roll over on her back the minute a cute guy like you walks into her apartment. A girl likes to be romanced a little. Why don't you romance me a little?"

"Like how?"

"Like this."

She gave me a gentle kiss. At least it started out as a gentle kiss. It didn't quite wind up that way. It wound up like an oral rape.

She wrapped her arms around me and closed me up in a bear hug that put all of her very close to all of me. Her breasts came through my back and her tongue did things to my mouth that hadn't been done to it in a long time.

44

Rosie was quite a kisser. Usually I like to lead but with her I didn't have a chance. Her tongue pried my lips apart and flitted into my mouth like a hopped-up hummingbird, and all the while she was holding me so tight against her that I couldn't breathe. Not that I wanted to. I was happy just the way I was.

She let go of the bear hug and I found out what air was like again. But it was only the beginning. One hand dropped to my thigh and she began to fool around a little. She played games with me and showed me a few little tricks that Mata Hari must have been pretty proud of. I grabbed her again and this time she didn't tell me to take it easy, and I didn't.

I got a hand into that pink silk nonsense and took hold of her breast. It was a nice breast to take hold of. I tried to cup it but my hand wasn't big enough.

So I used both hands. I mean, what the hell. I'm an easy guy to get along with.

She liked it when I touched her there. She started letting out these cute little moans and her hot little hands learned some new tricks on the spot. Me, I was having the time of my life. I've always been inordinately fond of breasts and she had plenty of breast to be fond of.

I got inspired and went to town. Pretty soon the silk fluff was a tangled mess on the floor and neither of us could have cared less. I shoved her down on the couch and crouched over her, my mouth busy with her breasts. She was squirming all over the place now, her moans shaking the walls and her eyes clenched tightly shut in the agony of passion.

My hands were all over her. I found a spot on the inside of her thigh that set her off completely. All I had to do was touch her there and she started shaking like an aspen in a tornado and moaning like a Siamese cat in heat.

When I kissed her there, my lips working like sixty, neither of us could take it any more. She told me where the bedroom was and we headed in that direction. I don't know why we bothered. We could have done it right in the middle of the living room floor and neither of us would have minded it a bit.

But we found the bedroom. The bed was a huge affair with a brass bedstead and all, and she fell on top of it as if she had been shot with a medium-size cannon. I got my clothes off. Please don't ask me how. I will always regard it as one of the major accomplishments of my life.

I was standing there, naked as a jaybird, and she was lying there, naked as a jaybird. She was also panting like a truck horse and, as I mentioned before, shaking like an aspen in a hurricane and moaning like a Siamese cat in heat. Her arms were at her sides, her hands balled up into tight fists.

I grinned like a Cheshire cat.

"Ted?"

It came out in a moan and I grinned some more.

"Ted?"

The grin spread.

"What are you going to do, Ted?"

I said: "I'm going to get into something more comfortable."

It was weird and wild and wicked and wonderful. She was a big girl and her body was a warm cushion, a hot pillow that tossed me to the top of the world and back again. She started moaning when it began and the moans got so loud that at one point I was afraid the ceiling was going to come down on us.

Her nails dug holes in my back.

I was a prisoner in a huge fortress of breasts and thighs and acres of female flesh. I was captive in a sexual jail, a willing slave, a condemned man eating a hearty meal. I moved and she moved and the motions were a primitive dance to a hungry god.

It was incredible.

For a while there I didn't think it was ever going to stop. Day turned to night, night turned back to day, and the whole process kept repeating like a spinning yin and yang sign. I felt as though I was being devoured whole, eaten alive and digested and assimilated into the body of this unbelievable woman. Rosie. Sweet Rosie. My little Rosie, with one hell of a yen for men.

It got better, and it got even better, and it got better yet.

And still better.

And then it ended.

I felt like Samson, but with a haircut. I sprawled on top of her like a sack of mashed potatoes, the sweat gushing out of me in a steady stream, my heart beating a mile and a half a minute and my eyelids weighted down with sacks of cement.

I tried to roll away from her.

But she wouldn't let me.

"More," she said. "Don't stop, Ted. You can't stop now."

"That's what you think."

"More!"

She was asking the impossible. If there was one thing in the world which I did not feel like doing it was what we had just finished doing. I was exhausted. Hell, I wasn't as young as I used to be. I couldn't take much more.

Besides, I was out of practice. I mean, what the hell. Enough is enough.

But evidently enough was not enough. Not for her, anyhow. Her hands got busy and her mouth got busy and her whole body started performing indescribable tricks, and pretty soon we were having another go at it, as the English might put it. I didn't want to, but I couldn't help myself.

And away we went.

I was beginning to see what Carl meant when he warned me against her. Good old Carl. He knew more than drinking and cooking. He knew women, God bless him. He knew which ones to stay away from.

I should have listened to him.

For awhile I strongly suspected that my death was just a few minutes ahead of me. My heart was pounding, my head was reeling and the spots in front of my eyes had spots in front of them.

And then it too was over.

This time I couldn't move at all. I just lay there in a pool of our sweat — it was impossible at this point to tell whose sweat was whose — and when I tried to raise my arm I couldn't. My arm knew better. It stayed right where it was.

But Rosie wasn't finished yet.

"More," she begged. It was ridiculous, but she actually expected me to make love to her a third time without a break. It was out of the question and I didn't even have the strength to explain to her what a silly notion it was.

I guess explanations wouldn't have done any good anyway. She was determined.

If I had had the strength I think I would have laughed. The whole idea now was so funny it deserved a good laugh. But I didn't have the strength. I just stayed right where I was.

And then she did something I had heard of and read about but had never before experienced. It was the absolute ultimate in sensation and it was totally unlike anything, any time, anywhere.

It worked.

The third time was bad. That doesn't do it justice. Actually, it was horrible.

I didn't have my heart in it but this didn't seem to bother Rosie in the least. I did have another portion of my anatomy in it and that was all she cared about. I went through my paces with the enthusiasm of a schoolboy for intermediate algebra and the interest of a fifty-year-old whore at the end of a busy day.

When it was over all I could think of was getting out of that room before she killed me. I was drained, utterly and totally and thoroughly and completely drained, used up and empty and exhausted. I didn't even want to think about women. I just wanted to stay away from them.

I got up and started finding my clothes. Then I turned around, and there was Rosie.

She had that look in her eye.

That hungry look.

And, at this stage of the game, she was one hell of a lot stronger than I was.

I still don't like to think about what might have happened if I hadn't been lucky. I might have remained at Rosie Ryan's posh little pad for the rest of my life, however long that may have been. I have visions of an extra room in her apartment, a room filled to overflowing with the skeletons of other men who couldn't get away in time.

But I did get lucky. I called upon what very little strength remained and swung, and I caught her with a lucky punch from somewhere north of third base. She had a glass jaw or something — whatever it was she went down like a ton of wet bricks and made a tired little heap in the middle of the bed-room rug.

I covered her with a blanket and left her there.

Getting out of the building was a hard job. It was a good thing they had an elevator or I never would have made it. As it was I had a hell of a time, but eventually there I was, facing the early morning on West 69th Street with drawn eyes and a haggard look on my face.

A cab passed, or started to until I hailed it. Taking a taxi a scant four blocks may strike you as startlingly stupid, but then you never went three rounds with Rosie Ryan.

It was the best investment I ever made.

The meter read forty cents when we landed in front of my humble home. I gave the driver a buck and told him to keep the change, which surprised him no end, let me tell you. Then I crawled up three flights of stairs to my own little room.

For a few long seconds I just stood there and stared lovingly at my bed. What the hell, it was just a bed. Not much of one, frankly. Just a single bed, no headboard, no footboard, just a rickety spring and sagging mattress.

It looked like Paradise.

So what if it was a broken-down wreck of a bed. So what if it only got made once a week when Mrs. Murdock saw fit to change the sheets.

It was mine.

All mine.

Mine alone.

And on that happy note I crawled out of my clothing, fell headlong on the bed and slept like sleeping beauty for ten delicious hours.

I woke up to dark skies and a headache. Rain passed my window without a comment and made splashing noises on the street below. I slithered out of bed, wrapped up in a towel and trundled off to shave and shower.

The shower was in one of its bad moods. There was no middle ground — I had to take it either hell-hot or dry-ice-cold. There should have been a special faucet marked Lukewarm, but there wasn't. It was a shame.

I took it hell-hot first and let my life drain out of my open pores. Then I flipped the whatchamacallit and had myself an ice bath that tightened the pores up like a paranoid virgin. The combination of the two restored my soul in some incomprehensible fashion and by the time I was dried and dressed and back in my room I felt almost human again. The effects of Rosie had by no means worn off — I was beginning to wonder if a total recovery was possible within the limits of a single lifetime — but I did feel a hell of a lot better. There was no denying that much.

I sat on the bed and looked at the wall like the catatonic Dr. Strom had warned me I was likely to turn into if I didn't watch myself. I didn't feel catatonic, just contemplative. It seemed like a natural time to contemplate. I certainly didn't have any sexual desires to sidetrack me. I didn't have any sexual desires at all, not after the morning's roll in the hay. Roll, hell. It was more like a double cartwheel in the hay. With bells on.

Contemplation.

Too many years back to think about I had read or heard or doped out the way to get your mind working in regular channels. You had to figure out and enumerate, first of all, all your immediate and future goals. Then, once they were all down on paper, you figured out steps to achieve them. You wrote those down as well, and then you went to work.

Simple, but important. More useful than it sounds, also more difficult to do. But I was determined. Life was a little too stagnant just then and Ted Lindsay was getting to the stage where he was bored with himself.

So I found a pencil and a hunk of paper and wrote at the top: *Eventually I want —*

Well, what did I want? Money in the bank, of course. Every red-blooded American boy wants money in the bank. If you don't want money in the bank there's something wrong with you. I read that somewhere, I think. It was in a booklet put out by a bank.

Anyway, I wanted it. So at the end of the column I wrote:
1. Money in the bank.

I thought about it, decided that was too vague, and changed it a little:
1. Fifty thousand dollars in the bank.

That was a nice round sum. I don't know exactly why I hit on it, but it had a good substantial feel to it. Poverty is not without its charm, but neither, for that matter, is money. I mean, what the hell.

What else? Well, I wanted to be successful, didn't I? Fifty thousand dollars would make me successful, but it wasn't just a matter of being successful. You have to be successful *at* something.

Newspapering? Making that kind of dough in the newspaper business is something that doesn't happen unless your name is Hearst. Mine isn't, and I'm glad of it.

The answer, then, was to make a wad of dough somehow — that would come in the second list — and then find the proper niche in the newspaper world. The proper niche? That was easy. It wasn't pounding a beat on a metropolitan daily. It wasn't swinging a desk or writing heads or rewriting or any of that nonsense. It was what half the newspapermen in the world spend their lives dreaming about. The other half, in case you wondered, spend their lives dreaming about being either foreign correspondent for the *New York Times* or editor of the Times, and they have as much chance of getting there as my half does.

I wrote:

2. Ownership of a small county weekly in the middle of nowhere.

Now that was more like it. Settling down in some godforsaken town in the state of Atrophy, putting a paper out once a week, writing news the way I wanted it written and saying the kinds of things I wanted to say in the editorial column. Getting back to the printshop and getting ink on my hands once in a while. Setting type and making up the paper on the stone and selling ads and sending out bills and working up circulation campaigns and all the myriad of tasks that are the sole responsibility of the poor dumb son of a bitch who happens to own the tiny little paper that nobody reads anyway.

It was what I wanted. And, therefore, it belonged on the list.

There was one thing more. It was dream time, and I was the unbeautiful dreamer of the beautiful dream, and only one item remained to make the dream complete. It didn't make much sense to put it on the list, but then it didn't make a hell of a lot of sense to have the list in the first place if you want to get technical about it.

I didn't want to get technical about it. I wrote, printing very carefully:

3. A wife and kids.

A wife who loved me all the way, the kind of wife who would be a complete wife, who wouldn't grow away from me, who wouldn't disappear some fine night with a nameless, faceless bastard and wind up in a smoking ruin of a car at the foot of an ugly ominous cliff. A wife who would help with the paper and cry when I was sad and laugh when I was happy, a wife who would have children for me and keep the house nice and make mad and passionate love and sleep by my side every night.

When you dream you might as well go all the way. But that's the whole point of writing it down. That way it isn't just a dream — it's there on paper when you're done mooning over it and you can't just look away and forget it. It had worked before — one fine day I made a list and two days later landed my first newspaper job, a copyboy slot on the *Louisville Courier*. A year later I was on the *Times*, and a year after that I had a desk of my own.

And, I swore up and down, it was going to work again. Or my name was not Ted Lindsay.

It was all there in black and white — money, a business, a family. Now it was time to get some of the specifics on the list.

I wrote: *Now I have to* —

1. Find some foolproof scheme for getting money in a hurry.

That was going to take a little thought: If a person could just sit down with a pencil and paper and wind up with a hatful of money, nobody in the country would have to work for a living. That might be nice, but as sure as God made little green spiders there was more to it than that. I went on to the next point, the paper. I sat around for awhile but I couldn't think of anything more compelling than *Buy a newspaper*, and at the moment the only sort of newspaper I could buy was the kind you pick up at a candy store. Step two couldn't be solved until step one was all tied up with a pink ribbon.

Step three?

Hmmmmmmm.

I was beginning to get a message. It had no logic behind it, but there was an intuitive impulse that said the same thing over and over, and a reporter's intuition is the next best thing to a woman's intuition — much as, as a wag once remarked, a reporter is the next best thing to a woman. I'm not sure what the bastard meant by that. Let's forget it for the time being.

The intuitive impulse went along these lines. A certain doll had a whole bunch of things going. A certain doll was the key to a whole host of appealing possibilities. This babe could figure quite prominently in steps one and two and three.

Three guesses what chick I'm talking about.

Well, it wasn't Rosie Ryan.

Nor was it Grace.

It wasn't Mrs. Murdock either.

Give up?

The intuitive impulse said, over and over, *Get a line on Cinderella Sims.*

So, printing as neatly as any third-grader, I wrote on my list:

2. Get a line on Cinderella Sims.

I can't explain the intuitive impulse. Intuition, by definition, is illogical. Rather, it's extra-logical. There may well be logic involved, but if so it is a form of logic that operates without the knowledge of the human brain. An intuitive logic, if you will.

What the hell.

What had happened? I'll tell you what had happened. I was walking down the street, minding my business, when out of an orange-colored sky a girl came along who knocked me far enough out of orbit to make me take a flier with a sexed-up bomb like Rosie. There was an aura about this girl that was more than beauty and more than sex, a fascination that hovered over her like a halo, except, somehow, not like a halo at all.

Call it chemistry, or biology. Call it any damned thing you please, but there was a legitimate impulse telling me that the fascination meant that my path and Cinderella Sims' path had to cross, that she was the key to everything I wanted and that I, somehow, was the key to everything she needed. Call it stupidity, or insanity, or catatonia, in the language of the incomparable Dr. Strom. Call it whatever you damn well please, I believed it.

I went over to the window and stared through the rain at the basement window across the street. There didn't seem to be any lights on — either she wasn't home, or she was sleeping, or in the dead of night she had moved to Saudi Arabia. Still, looking at her window gave me something to do.

I stared so intently at the window that I did not hear the footsteps in the hallway.

Nor did I hear my door open.

But I heard the voice, sweet as honey, soft as dewdrops, malicious as a scandal sheet.

The voice said: "Put up your hands, Mr. Lindsay. And turn around. Slowly."

I put up my hands. I turned around, slowly.

And I caught my breath.

And stared.

There was rain in her hair and color in her cheeks. She was dressed in a man's flannel shirt and a pair of blue jeans but no man ever looked half so good in them. Her eyes were filled with fire and her pretty chest was heaving like mad, probably because the damned stairs were so damned steep.

There was a gun in her hand and it was pointed at the spot in my chest where my heart is supposed to be.

I will give you three guesses who she was. Not Rosie Ryan. Not Grace. Not Mrs. Murdock either.

The girl with her finger on the trigger was, inevitably, Cinderella Sims.

"Mr. Lindsay," she said. "Mr. Ted Lindsay. You'd better talk fast, Mr. Lindsay. You'd better tell me everything there is to tell me and you'd better do it in a hurry or so help me God I'll kill you."

"But—"

"I'm not kidding," she went on, her eyes burning and her hands trembling a little. If her hands trembled too much that howitzer she was pointing at me could go off, and if it went off it could make a perfect mess of the room. Hell, there would be blood all over the ratty carpet. My blood. And I had grown kind of attached to my blood over the years.

"You'd better explain, Mr. Lindsay. You've got a lot of explaining to do."

"I do?"

Her face hardened, if that was possible. For a second I was scared she wasn't going to give me a chance to explain. But what in the name of God was I supposed to explain?

"What should I explain?"

"How you found me, Mr. Lindsay. Why you're after me. Who you are. Whom you're working for. What the rest of them know about me."

She had to be insane. There was no other explanation for it—she simply had to be out of her mind. Either she was nuts or I was, and in a minute it wasn't going to make much difference which one of us had marbles missing. In another minute that gun was going to go off and I was going to turn into a not-too-vital statistic.

"Hey," I said. "Look. I mean, give me a chance to explain."

"Go ahead."

"I didn't do anything," I said. "I'm just a broken-down old reporter taking a rest cure in the big city. I'm not working for anybody. I mean, I sling hash at a diner on Columbus Avenue. Grace's Lunch. You can call them and ask them. They'll tell you."

She sighed.

"And I saw you yesterday for the first time, and I don't know anything about you, and I'm damned if I can understand why you're holding a gun on me, and—"

She sighed again.

"Look, I—"

"Mr. Lindsay." she said. "Mr. Lindsay, the sight of me yesterday afternoon was enough to stagger you. You recognized me, and I must say you were obvious enough about it. Then you followed me."

That much was true. I followed her, all right. Like a rat following the Pied Piper. But what in hell—

"Then you started investigating," she went on. "Checking the nameplate in the hall. Sneaking subtle glances through my window. Keeping my apartment under constant surveillance from the building across the street. How can you deny it when I caught you in the act?"

I didn't even try to deny it. I was too busy wondering where they were going to ship the body. I'd made a big mistake, not giving Mrs. Murdock my Louisville address. They'd probably plant me in Potter's Field instead of sticking me in my native earth.

"I've waited long enough, Mr. Lindsay. Start talking. And you'd better make it good."

4

I made it good.

There was this book I read once called *The Screaming Mimi* written by a guy named Fredric Brown. It was about this newspaperman, you see, and I have always been partial to novels about newspapermen, much as I have always been partial to novels by Fredric Brown.

Anyway, at one point in this book this newspaperman is alone in a room with this girl, and this girl is out of her skull, as well as being out of her clothing, and in her hand there is this knife. In order to avoid getting this knife between his ribs, this newspaperman begins talking. Talk, it seems, keeps this girl from doing much of anything, such as stabbing this newspaperman. He talks about everything under or over the sun, quotes Shakespearean soliloquies, rattles off farm prices, anything so long as he doesn't stop talking. And finally someone comes and takes the girl away, and all is well, and that is that.

Which, more or less, is what I did. Since I didn't know just where to start I started at the beginning, and if I left anything out I can't remember what it might have been. I told her everything there was to tell about me and Mona and Louisville and Grace's Lunch and oriental philosophy and God knows what else. Somewhere along the way I managed to talk her out of pulling the trigger, though just what it was that I mentioned that did the trick is something I'm afraid I will never know. Whatever it was, it worked, and I will be forever thankful to it.

Oh, yes. There was one part I didn't bother recounting to her. I left out Rosie. For some reason I didn't think she would understand, and even if she did, I wasn't altogether proud of my participation in that particular bedroom farce. By all rules I acquitted myself nobly in that little battle of the sexes, but it wasn't the sort of thing I wanted to dwell on.

I finished, finally, and I looked at her, timidly, and the gun was no longer centered upon my chest. It was pointing at the floor.

I felt a good deal better about the whole thing.

First she lowered the gun; then she lowered her eyes. "I'm sorry, Mr. Lindsay," she said, her voice one hell of a lot softer now, her tone downright apologetic. "It seems I've made a mistake. But it was a logical mistake. I have to be very careful."

I started to tell her what the hell, mistakes happen, it's all in the game. Then it occurred to me that maybe it was my turn to seize the advantage and push a little. After all, it was my room she was standing in with a cannon in her fist. If anyone had the right to demand an explanation, I did.

I said: "Your turn."

She just looked at me.

"You came in here with a gun," I told her. "You pointed that gun at me and scared me out of several years' growth. And I'm a growing boy. Or at least I was."

"But—"

"So it's your turn to talk. It's your turn to tell me just what in hell is making you so suspicious about everything. I think I have a right to know."

She pursed her lips and I waited. Her hair was lovely now, the water making it all sleek and shiny, and her eyes had a feathery softness to replace the fire that had been in them when the gun was aimed at me.

"No," she said finally. "It wouldn't interest you."

"Try me."

"It's not important," she said. "I made a mistake and I'm sorry. Can't we let it go at that?"

"No."

"Pardon?"

"No, we can't let it go at that. I want to get to the bottom of this, dammit. You'd better explain."

"And if I don't?"

"I'll take the gun away from you and spank your behind for you."

She looked at me. "You know," she said after a minute, "I believe that's just what you'd do. That's just the sort of thing a man like you might do."

"So do I get the brass ring?"

"Pardon?"

"Are you going to tell me what all this nonsense is about?"

"Well," she said thoughtfully. "Well, I guess I have to, don't I?"

I took the gun from her, looked at it cautiously, sniffed at the barrel the way the police always do in the movies and dropped it into the bureau drawer. Once the gun was in the drawer and the drawer shut I felt one hell of a lot better. Guns make me nervous.

Then I made her sit down on the bed, found a cigarette for her and a cigarette for me and lit both of them. I sat down on the chair — which no longer faced her window, but faced her instead — and took a deep drag on my cigarette. It was her show now and I waited for her to say something.

It took her a while, and while I waited I could see how nervous she was. There was one hell of a lot of tension inside that pretty little body and it would probably be a good idea for her to talk some of it out. I was ready to listen. That was me — Lend-an-ear Lindsay, always willing and able to help out a damsel in distress.

"I'm in trouble," she said. "Bad trouble."

"Police trouble?"

She hesitated, then shook her head *no*.

"What kind?"

"Money trouble."

"There's another kind?"

She shrugged. "It's hard to explain, Mr. Lindsay."

"Ted."

"Ted. I don't know how to start."

"Just plunge in. And by the way, what do I call you? Cinderella Sims sounds too good to be true."

"It's my real name. People generally call me Cindy."

"Cindy Sims," I said, trying it out. It sounded fine. I liked it.

"There were six of them," she said, getting started again. "Five men and a girl. I had a job as a cashier at West of the Lake — that's a gambling joint at Tahoe in Nevada. It's called West of the Lake because there's Lake Tahoe and the club is to the west of it."

"Go on."

"They were a confidence mob. You know, con men. Only I didn't know it at the time. I thought they were just a party of tourists. That's what they told me and I didn't see any reason why it should be anything else. They said they were playing a practical joke on this other guy but they were actually trying to bilk him. I didn't find this out until later."

I digested this. She put out her cigarette and went on a little further.

"The man's name was McGuire. I don't know what he did. He was from Texas and I think somebody said he was an oil-man or something. Everybody from Texas is an oilman. At least it seems that way. One of the men, a man named Eddie Reed, came to me and told me they were playing a joke on McGuire. They were offering him phony chips at a discount for him to turn in. He'd come in, buy a few thousand dollars' worth of chips, fool around at the roulette wheel, and then cash the stack."

"So?"

"So he would come in with chips that he hadn't paid for. Say he comes in with three thousand dollars' worth in his pocket, buys another three thousand worth, and breaks even on the wheel. When he cashes I give him six thousand. He's three thousand ahead, minus what he has to pay for the chips."

I thought it over. "Okay," I said. "It doesn't make sense. You can't make phony chips that pass a Vegas house. They work pretty hard on monogram and color and everything else in the book. Those chips are as individual as fingerprints. I don't get it."

She grinned. "Neither did McGuire," she said. "And the girl—she was a busty blonde named Lori Leigh—she kept him from getting much of anything, except what she had to offer. She was working with them from the inside, living with McGuire and wearing him out at night so that he couldn't think straight during the day. I found this out later, you see. I didn't understand any of it at the time. I thought it was a joke, the way Eddie Reed said it was."

"Okay," I said. "Go on."

"The thing about the chips," she said, "is that you couldn't tell them from real ones."

"I don't believe it."

"Let me finish. You couldn't tell them from real ones because they were real ones. Reed and the others had bought them from the house and hadn't bothered to cash them in. Now do you see it?"

"No."

"I'm glad, because neither did I. Not then. You see, Reed told me it was all a joke on McGuire. They were pretending to give him this method of cheating the house, when actually the house wasn't losing a nickel. Reed wanted me to act like everything was perfectly okay when McGuire cashed in his chips. I was supposed to take it in stride if he seemed nervous or anything, instead of pushing the panic button the way we're supposed to if something seems strange."

"So?"

She stroked her chin. "Now it gets complicated."

"It can't get any more complicated than it already is."

"It does, though. Want to hear more?"

"Go on."

"After McGuire and Lori Leigh were steady bed partners, Reed got to work on McGuire. Played the slots next to him and got to talking with him. He played it just right, made McGuire look like a big man in front of the girl and McGuire ate it all up. They had dinner a couple times and Reed let it slip that it didn't matter how much he gambled, he couldn't lose anything. McGuire wanted to know why and Reed told him how he bought perfect fakes at fifty cents on the dollar. That way he had to come out ahead, even with the normal house percentage against the player."

"And McGuire bit?"

"Evidently. He kept asking Reed to let him in on it. He was the kind of gambler who doesn't belong in a house, always looking for a little of the best of it. He liked to gamble, but he liked it better if he couldn't lose."

"I know the type."

"So did Reed. After awhile he let himself be persuaded to buy some chips for McGuire. McGuire really had to talk hard to get him to agree. He was so completely sold it was ridiculous."

"Keep talking."

"Reed sold McGuire a hundred dollars' worth of chips, ones he'd bought himself at the house a few days back. McGuire played with them, came out as little ahead, and cashed them in. They were perfectly legitimate, so naturally I cashed them. That was easy enough."

"And?"

"More of the same. Next night it was two hundred bucks' worth and McGuire was really getting hungry. He was loaded, but that kind of guy never has as much money as he'd like to have. He wanted more and he must have figured this gimmick as a steady source of income."

"I think I'm beginning to get it."

"From here on it's simple. McGuire wants to buy a big load of fifty and hundred buck chips. Reed says he can't handle the deal himself but he knows the men who can. Naturally they're other members of the con mob. Reed makes the contact and they agree to let McGuire have a hundred thousand worth, cash in advance. McGuire figures to stay in Vegas the rest of his life, gamble every night and come out ahead every night."

"He must have rocks in his head. A man can't lose every night and cash out a winner every night without the management figuring which end is up."

"Of course not. But don't forget McGuire had Lori keeping his bed warm. He wasn't in condition to think straight. Besides, he was convinced he could win money on his own hook. He had a system for roulette. Everybody does."

I sighed.

"Okay," I said. "They've got McGuire forking over fifty grand for a hundred grand worth of fake chips which, obviously, don't exist. What do they do next? Just skip town? I suppose it would work but it might be pretty sloppy."

She shook her head. "They were cuter than that," she said. "Reed left and the guy who was supposed to be swinging the deal also left. Another guy, the one who was supposed to be partners in the deal, stayed with McGuire. Then two other guys break in."

"Also part of the con mob?"

"Of course. Only they're posing as police officers. They say they've overheard the whole thing, Reed and the other one are in jail, and they've come to arrest the partner—his name was Finch—and, also, McGuire."

"Keep talking."

"Finch explains that he and McGuire don't know anything about it, that they got roped in without understanding the setup. The cop starts to soften and Finch pushes it. He offers a bribe. One cop wants to take the money and the other one doesn't. They put on a nice little act until the "decent" cop comes out ahead. Finch makes the payoff, flashes a roll and pays off both the cops. This makes it look better than if they asked McGuire for the money."

"I get it."

"Then the cops do it up brown. They explain that they're going to have to pretend that Finch and McGuire skipped before they got there. They warn the two of them to stay out of Nevada for the rest of their lives, that they're safe as long as they stay out of the state because their prints and pictures won't go on the wire. The cops walk out, Finch goes to his room and McGuire, an honorable man, gets his wallet and pays Finch half the bribe money."

"And that's it?"

"That's it."

"Doesn't McGuire whine for his fifty thousand?"

"How can he? He's wanted for fraud and a million other things. The people who took his money are supposedly under arrest and his money's supposedly impounded by the police. If he does tumble to the whole thing, by that time everybody connected with it is a million miles away spending McGuire's money."

It was perfect, almost too perfect. It was based on the fundamental principle underlying every con game in the world — find a mark who wants a fast buck, make him work his way in hard, let him win a little at the start; play him along, let him sell himself on the one big deal that will set him up for life, get his stake and blow him off neatly so that he can't bitch to the law.

I smoked another cigarette and thought about it. It could work — and, evidently, it *had* worked. It wouldn't take on just anybody — you needed a mark who was dumber than most. But, as Barnum put it, there's one born every minute.

It was lovely.

McGuire was left completely on the hook. His money was gone and he didn't know who had taken it or how to get it back. The only two people he knew were Lori and Reed, and neither of them wound up with the dough. And he'd be in such a hell of a rush to get out of town that he wouldn't even stop to think about them.

Fifty thousand dollars. It was a lot of dough. And, I realized with a start, it was the precise amount on my list. *Fifty thousand dollars in the bank.* That's what it said, right there at the top of the list.

Lovely.

I killed my cigarette and looked across at her. Her face was expressionless, her eyes empty, her mouth neither smiling nor frowning. I wondered just where she fit in, whether she was lying or telling the truth, how she knew so much and what in the name of the Lord she was afraid of. There didn't seem to be anything for her to worry about, for God's sake. All she did was play patsy in an unassuming sort of a way, and even so she hadn't done anything the least bit illegal.

And she was certainly afraid. You don't throw a gun on a total stranger for the pure hell of it. She was scared green.

I wondered why.

"That's it," she said. "The whole bit from beginning to end. Now do you understand?"

"Almost. There's one point I'm a little unclear on. Maybe you can straighten me out."

Her eyebrows went up.

"The con game itself is easy enough to understand. It's a new one on me but it makes sense."

"What doesn't?"

"You."

She looked very puzzled.

"You," I repeated. "For one thing, how in hell do you know all this if all they told you was the cover story? Secondly, what's your part in the whole thing? Why aren't you back cashing chips at West of the Lake or whatever the hell it is?"

She started laughing.

"Look, I—"

Loud laughter, her breasts rising and falling in a delicious sort of way, her eyes filling with tears. I guess the laughter was a valve opening up so that she could let off steam and ease some of the tension. I didn't mind. If she wanted to laugh it was okay with me.

"Ted," she said. "Oh my God."

"Well?"

"I didn't tell you that part," she said. "The most important part of all and I left you in the dark."

"So turn on the lights."

"The most important part. The reason I've bothered telling you the whole thing, and I leave out the most important part of all. It's silly."

"Look, Cindy. Tell me."

She smiled.

"Come on."

"Could I have a cigarette?"

I gave her a cigarette.

"Light?"

I lit hers, then took one of my own.

"Ted," she said, blowing out smoke. "Poor Ted. You don't understand."

"The suspense," I said, "is killing me."

"Ted," she said. "I have the money in my room. In a little black satchel. All the money. Fifty thousand dollars in twenty dollar bills and it's all mine!"

I did not take it like a man. I took it like a low blow. I sagged in the middle, doubled up in something quite close to agony and flopped from my chair to the floor. I felt as though someone had run over me with a garbage scow. I know people don't get run over with garbage scows, not unless they make a practice of swimming the East River. But that's how I felt.

"I took it," she said breathlessly. "We all met in the hotel room and I got out of there with the money. The joke was on them — all the work they put into the job, and little Cindy Sims walked off with the boodle. The joke was sure as hell on them."

"How?" I croaked.

"Just picked it up, picked it up and walked off with it. They never even suspected. Never tumbled to it for a minute. They thought I was some kind of a moron, a nice chick to have around the place but nothing to worry about. I guess they know better now, the bastards."

"Wait," I said. "Hold on a minute. How did you find out about it all?"

"It was easy, Ted. Too easy."

"How?"

"Ed Reed," she said. "The little bastard who worked on McGuire. The oily, slimy, slick-talking son of a bitch. He told me all about it."

"Why in hell should he —"

"He was bragging, Ted. It made him feel like a big shot. He was a sucker the same way as McGuire was."

"But why you?"

"Because I was sleeping with him."

It hurt. It shouldn't have hurt — she was just some lonely frail who had blown in out of the night, but still it hurt. I don't know what I suspected — a virgin, maybe, although virginity had never been my particular kick. I won't even try to analyze it. It hurt.

"It was horrible, Ted. He picked me up pretty skillfully and he was lots of fun at first — a big spender, a happy sort of a guy if you didn't notice what went on behind the mask. Later I learned to notice. But not at first.

"Then, after the first trip to bed, he got ugly. He wanted me to do…unnatural things. Things I didn't like. They make me sick to my stomach to think about them. You know the things fairies do to each other?"

I nodded.

"Those things. And worse. He wanted me to whip him, to hurt him. It was all pretty sickening."

"But you did it."

She nodded. "By this time I knew the swindle. I already had my mind made up, Ted. I was getting my share. I was going to wind up with the dough."

"And you did."

"So I did."

I looked at the bundle of innocence sitting on my bed and thought of the bundle of money in her room, thought of the cold blood under that warm exterior, of the mind and the body and the money and a few other things. I thought of what it must have been like with her and Reed in bed. It must have been pretty unpleasant for her, although it must have been pretty goddamned great for Reed, damn him. I envied him. I envied anybody who had something like Cinderella Sims in bed with him.

She would be good, damned good. I stared hard at her, saw the way the top half of her made a man's flannel shirt stretch all out of shape, saw the way her behind was snug and tight in the dungarees.

And, evidently, there was something left that Rosie Ryan hadn't managed to drain out of me altogether. Because I wanted Cindy, wanted her desperately, wanted her inside and out with a want that was more than mere sex, although there was sure as hell a lot of pure sex mixed in with whatever else was there. I wanted her and it must have shown in my eyes because I could read an answer in her eyes, an answer that said she knew what I was thinking.

"So you got the money," I said. I didn't particularly feel like talking but I forced it. "So you got the money. Where does the problem come in?"

"They're after me."

"The law?"

She shook her head. "As far as the law is concerned, no crime was ever committed. Nobody complained. McGuire certainly won't complain."

"The con mob?"

"Of course. They went to a lot of trouble for this one, spent one hell of a lot of money getting things set up properly. And they're not the type of people who let their dough slide down the drain. That's not the way they play. They'll hound me forever and kill me if they get a chance. And I don't particularly feel like dying, Ted. I'm too young for that."

"Do they know where you are?"

"I don't know. Reed has contacts everywhere. He's got more connections than a plumber, the dirty son of a bitch. I thought you were one of his contacts when you spotted me. That's why I had to come up and hold a gun on you. I almost killed you, almost shot you in the back. But I had to find out first whether or not you'd gotten in touch with Reed yet. It's good I asked."

"No kidding."

"I think he knows I'm in New York. He knows me under another name—that's why I went back to my old name here, Cinderella Sims. That's not the name I was working under in Tahoe."

"What are you going to do?"

"I don't know."

"No ideas at all?"

She shrugged. "Ideas are cheap. I had a million ideas at first and none of them panned out. I was going to jump the border for Mexico and stay there. He'd never even bother looking down there. I'd be safe."

"Why didn't you go?"

"I don't know. God, from the minute I grabbed that money everything started to go wrong. I got to the airport and took the first flight out. It happened to go to New York. That's why I'm here."

"Why don't you fly down to Mexico?"

"I waited too long. Now I'm sure they know I'm in New York. I'm scared stiff. I've been living here for a month now and I've been at five different addresses in that time. At first I stayed in a hotel but then I figured it was too easy to be seen that way. Now I'm living across the street. I won't even go downtown, just stay in the neighborhood and keep in my room as much as I can. I don't dare stay here for more than a week."

"Because you might be spotted?"

She nodded soberly.

"It's rough."

"I'm scared," she said. "I've never been afraid like this and every day it gets worse. It's silly — fifty thousand dollars and I don't even dare enjoy it. I can't go shopping, can't do anything. I just sit around and go out of my mind."

I put out my cigarette.

"Ted," she said. "Ted, I told you all this for a reason. I need help."

"What kind of help?"

"I don't even know. I just know I need somebody who can figure out a way for us to get clear with the money so that I don't have to keep on running like this for the rest of my life. I can't take much more of this. It's wearing me down. I have trouble sleeping, it's getting so bad."

"You think I can help?"

"We stand a better chance with two of us. I won't have to go out any more, for one thing. And they don't know you. That gives me a cover right there."

I thought about it.

"I'll give you half," she said. "Twenty-five thousand, if we get out of this. It's worth it to me. I just can't stand the running any more. You get me out of this and half the money's yours."

I got up from the chair. My head was starting to reel a little and my feet weren't quite as steady as the Rock of Gibraltar. But I made it over to the bed and sat down next to her.

I could smell her. She smelled as though she'd just had a bath, fresh and clean and sweet.

72

"Is it a deal, Ted?"

I thought about it. Twenty-five thousand dollars was one hell of a lot of money. I was buying trouble but the price seemed to be right.

Almost right, anyway.

"I want more," I heard my self saying.

"Isn't half enough? My God, Ted — that's a lot of money. I want some left for myself."

"The money's fine. That's not what I meant. I want what Eddie Reed was getting. I want you in bed."

She looked up at me and her eyes were shiny with laughter. "Ted," she said. "Ted, Ted, Ted. That part of it goes without saying."

"When do we start?"

She grinned.

"Here we are," she said, "and here's a bed. It's been a long time, Ted. Let's seal the bargain."

I reached for her.

5

When I kissed her, her hands went around me at once, holding me close. Her arms weren't tight around me but pressed me close with a gentleness matched only by the feeling of her mouth on mine. Her lips were softer than the rain in her hair and her mouth tasted of nectar and ambrosia.

The first kiss was like that all the way — firm but yielding, gentle and tender but still thoroughly satisfying, exciting and oddly chaste all at once. We kissed with our mouths closed, which was something I had almost forgotten how to do, and it was nice.

I let go of her; looked at her. She smiled with her lips and eyes, the shy smile of a schoolgirl. There was something frighteningly virginal about her and I had to force myself to remember that this was the girl who had slept with Eddie Reed and had then made off with a boodle of fifty grand. It seemed impossible.

The second kiss was different. This time my tongue licked at her lips and they parted for me. Her arms were tight around me and genuine passion was pushing the virginal quality into the background. I forced my tongue deep into the hidden recesses of her mouth, tasting the overwhelming sweetness of her, holding her tight against me and feeling her soft warm breasts against my chest.

She went limp when the kiss ended. I took her lovely face in my hands and started kissing her all over it—her eyelids, her cheeks, her little ears, the tip of her little nose. She made purring noises like a fat cat on a thick rug in front of a warm fire.

I kissed her throat, her hair, the nape of her neck. I could feel the passion growing in her and could feel my own passion growing to meet it. Her skin was soft, very soft, and her hair smelled sweet as new-mown hay.

We didn't talk. She stretched out on my bed and I lay down beside her, still kissing her. Our mouths met and I lay right on top of her, feeling her beneath me. This time her tongue darted into my mouth and her warm body started to move below me.

I ran my hands over her. I liked the feel of her under my hands. I wanted to keep touching her forever until we both went up in smoke.

"Ted—"

I looked into her eyes.

"Take off my clothes, Ted."

My fingers were trembling but I forced them to behave. I unbuttoned all the buttons on the man's flannel shirt and slipped it back over her shoulders. She wasn't wearing a bra and the sudden sight of her perfect breasts was almost too much for me. I could only look at them. My fingers itched to touch them but all I could do was stare.

She propped herself up on her elbows and I got the shirt off and let it fall to the floor. With an effort I got out of my own shirt and tossed it away too. Then I lay down on top of her again and we were both naked from the waist up, our flesh touching, our bodies straining to get us as close together as possible.

"You've got hair on your chest," she said. "I'm glad. I like it, Ted. I like the way it feels against me."

I moved so that the hair on my chest brushed the tips of her breasts and she shook like a leaf. Her eyes were clenched shut and her lips were parted.

I took her breasts in my hands and stroked them. I never knew anything could be so soft, so smooth, so firm and so perfect. I ran my lips over each breast in turn, tasting the flavor of her, kissing the firm pink nipples that stood up like little toy soldiers.

And she was making noises now. Her breathing filled the whole room.

I unbuttoned her dungarees and worked them over her hips. They were tight on her and it was tough getting them off. I pulled off her tennis shoes without untying them and rolled down her socks, slipping them from her feet.

She was wearing white silk panties and I could see right through them.

Then she wasn't wearing anything at all.

She was a goddess, a vision, a dream. She was the one perfect woman in the whole imperfect world and she was mine, all mine. I touched her belly and the insides of her full thighs. I stroked her buttocks and cupped them in my hands, squeezing them gently.

I touched her everywhere and she went completely wild.

"Now, Ted! I can't wait another minute. Hurry up, Ted. Please!"

I got my clothes off and let them stay where they landed. I hurled myself upon her, my blood pounding in my ears, my heart beating at an impossible speed, my whole body pulsing and aching for her. The sensation of her body under my body was indescribable. I let the rapture of it wash over me like a scented bath.

When it began she let out a little gasp of pain and pleasure. Her arms were bands of steel now and her legs wound around me like creeping vines. Her body tossed in the rhythm of love and her moans gradually increased in volume until they drowned out everything else in the entire world. I thought I would go out of my mind and I didn't care if I did.

It was raining outside but I couldn't hear it. The bed was squealing like a stuck pig, unaccustomed to the workout it was getting. But I didn't hear that either.

All I could hear was Cindy.

The world went black as night, then turned the color of white-hot lead. It was not day, not night, no point in time at all. It was a disc spinning in Limbo, a solar eclipse at high noon, the whole wonderful world standing on its ear and singing at the top of its sturdy young lungs. It was heaven and hell, night and day.

It kept going on, and it kept getting better and better and better, and there was a time when I thought we were both going to die just as we were, locked together for all time. They would have to bury us locked in the position of love because no force on earth could drag us apart. And that wouldn't be half bad. There were lots worse ways of spending eternity.

When it happened it was a little like dying. There was a clap of thunder that came not from the heavens but from us, and there was the absolute ultimate in sensation and joy, and I felt like screaming at the top of my lungs. Maybe I did. I know Cindy did.

There was the peak, and it happened for both of us at once. Then there was the descent, slow and beautiful, quite perfect, with muscles going slack and mouths gulping air and bodies limp as noodles. There was sweat, a lot of it, and there was no tension at all anywhere in the world.

We lay together for a long time and then I left her, flopping flat on my back with my eyes staring vacantly at the ceiling. I could hear us breathing but that was all I could hear.

Several eternities later she reached out a hand to touch my face. I kissed the tips of her fingers, then said her name in a voice that did not sound like mine at all.

"Ted," she whispered. "God, that was good. Oh, God. You have no idea how much I needed that. I would have died without it, I think. And it was so good. So wonderfully amazingly good."

I didn't say anything. I didn't have to. She had said it all.

I closed my eyes. I thought about the girl and the money and, strangely, of Dr. Strom. He didn't know all the answers after all. This was the therapy I needed all along, the sure cure for anything under the sun. This was what I needed and now I had it.

Sleep came quickly.

We woke up a little after midnight. In theory it was time for me to go to work, but I had no intention of returning to Grace's Lunch then or ever after, not even to pick up my pay. We had fifty thousand dollars between us. We didn't have to work. I wasn't going to pour any more coffee, not for a hell of a long while.

We lay there, warm and naked, and we talked about things. I don't remember what we said. We babbled on about the little meaningless things that became very relevant to us in the sublime intimacy of love. She talked and I talked and I no longer recall a thing we said.

Then we made love.

It was different this time — not better, not worse, but different. Now it was the union of two bodies that knew one another, two bodies joining like a reunion of old army buddies, and it was slow and gentle, lazy and languorous, with a passion beneath it all that was almost terrifying in its potency. When it was over the glow lasted a long time and I felt better than I'd ever felt before in my life.

Then: "Ted?"

"Mmmmm?"

"I'm hungry. How about you?"

"Now that you mention it—"

"I'm starving. Let's get a bite to eat."

I thought about it. "I don't know," I said. "I don't know if I can get up."

"Try."

I tried.

"Come on, Ted."

I sat up on the bed, then fell back down again. The next time I made it and we got dressed. When she was stepping into the underpants I gave her a little pinch in a very pinchable area and she purred again.

"Watch that," she said. "You might be biting off more than you can chew."

"I like the metaphor."

"Stinker. You know what I mean."

I knew what she meant.

I put on clean clothes and gave her one of my shirts in place of the man's shirt she'd been wearing. It was loose on her, but I liked the way it looked when she moved around. I felt like tossing her back on the bed and ripping the shirt off her but I wasn't sure I had the strength.

I opened a window to air the love-smell out of the room and we went downstairs and out of the building. The rain had given up and gone home to Jersey and the air was as clean as Cindy's hair. The pavement was still damp but starting to dry up; the air was warm. I looked around from the doorway but I couldn't see anybody anywhere and we took off down the street toward Broadway.

We found a coffee joint that was still open at that hour and got a booth near the back. The waitress was a tight-lipped old biddy who threw the silverware at us and got annoyed when we asked for menus. But the food was good and we were both starved.

Cindy had a plate of ham and eggs with a side of home fries and two cups of joe with plenty of cream and sugar. I settled on a stack of wheat cakes with a brace of little link sausages, drowned the mess in maple syrup and took my coffee black.

The food disappeared very quickly.

Then we talked. I lit cigarettes for both of us, got us each another cup of coffee, and got the ball rolling as soon as the waitress was out of earshot.

"Okay, Cindy. Where do we go from here?"

"I don't know."

"I suppose we've got to get out of town. If Reed knows you're here it's only a matter of time before he catches up with you. And there won't be much you can do. You can't turn to the police any more than he can."

She nodded.

"The only question is where. Any ideas?"

"I used to think about Mexico. But I don't know any more. I can't even think straight, Ted."

I did some thinking, gulped some coffee and smoked some of my cigarette. "Look," I said, "any place that's large, any place where people generally go, he's likely to turn up. Even if we leave the country there's a chance. Someplace like Mexico City, for example. People go there all the time. He might run into us."

"Europe?"

"Possibly. But even then we wouldn't be set up right. The money wouldn't last forever. It's a lot of money but after awhile it would be gone and we'd be stranded. We have to be somewhere where the money can work for us."

"I don't understand."

"Somewhere in the States," I said. "Somewhere where we can use the dough to get set up in a business that will take care of us. See what I mean? With a stake of fifty grand we can get up fairly high, high enough so that the money will make more money for us."

"You sound like a stockbroker."

"I'm serious," I said, trying to sound serious, working hard at it because now it was my turn to sell her on something and I had no idea how hard or easy it might turn out to be.

"Go on."

"A small town," I said, making it sound as though all of this was just occurring to me for the first time. "Out west, maybe. Arizona or New Mexico. We could just move in, settle down, buy a house. Get hold of a business of some sort, pay a lot down and arrange terms for the rest. Then we'd be safe, don't you see? We wouldn't be a couple of crooks on the lam. We'd be a nice solid respectable middle-class couple with a lot of dough and no worries."

She thought about it. Her face was a mask and I couldn't tell what she was thinking. "What kind of a business?" she wondered. "A store or something like that? Would you know anything about running it?"

"Not a store. Maybe a newspaper. I could probably buy a small weekly dirt cheap, make a go of it. We'd be the solidest citizens in creation. Lots of power, tight with the law, everything. It couldn't miss."

"Would it be that easy to find one for sale?"

"A cinch. Little papers turn over all the time. The price is high but the terms are easy if you've got enough cash to cover the down payment." I paused, counted three beats, and asked: "How does it sound to you?"

"I don't know."

I waited.

"I'm not the stay-at-home type, Ted. I've been on the go all my life. I might get bored with it, might want to hit the road. Then what do we do?"

"You mean if you want to split up?"

She nodded. "This is good," she said. "What you and I have now. But it might not last forever. Things like this never do, you know."

I had my own ideas about that. But I let it pass for the time being.

"You can leave anytime you want to," I told her, forcing the words out and trying not to remember how good it had been with her back in my room. "I wouldn't try to hold you. As soon as it's safe you can go whenever and wherever you please. That part's strictly up to you."

"And the money?"

"We split. Strictly down the middle. Whatever I have when it's time to split, you get half."

"Half the paper?"

"Half the paper — either a cash deal or a stock deal. That's simple enough. Or we could get married and then get a divorce with the alimony agreement set up so that you'd wind up with half."

"That sounds fair enough."

"I'd give it to you in writing, but — "

"Don't be silly," she said. "You could hardly put that sort of thing in writing, not now. Anyway, we have to trust each other all the way. If we don't we might as well throw it up right at the start."

I agreed with her.

"What now?"

"Back to bed," I said. "We'll get out of town in the morning, catch the first plane out of here to Arizona. Then I'll find out what papers are for sale and start lining up a deal. The first thing to do is to get out of town. We don't want Reed on our necks. It's hard enough without him."

She nodded and we got out of the restaurant. I paid the check and tipped the waitress on general principles and we tripped out of the restaurant and back toward her apartment. We'd decided on staying at her place instead of mine. She had a double bed, and the way we'd been behaving lately we could use extra room.

It was still a nice night on the way back. The lamp posts cast long shadows and the moon was a tiny crescent on the corner of a patch of black sky.

Then her hand was on my arm and her fingers were digging into me and she was dragging me into the doorway of a brick building maybe fifty yards from where we lived.

"Don't say a word," she whispered. "Don't even move. For God's sake."

I obeyed. I was too mixed up to breathe.

"Down the block," she said. "By the lamp post. You see him?"

I looked and saw him. He was a big man in a houndstooth jacket. He looked tough.

"Baron," she said, "Dick Baron. One of the phony cops. I almost missed him, dammit."

I couldn't breathe at all now.

"And Reed's across the street. There's the little bastard right now. We would have walked right into them. Oh, my God. Oh God in heaven."

"Easy, Cindy."

"They've got the place staked out. They know right where I am and they're waiting for me. God. Ted. Oh, God. What in God's name do we do now?"

"Easy," I said. "Take it easy. They had a trap for us but we spotted it. So the trap's a bust. We turn around and we walk away and we're safe. They can take their traps and shove them."

She looked at me, wide-eyed.

"We're clear," I said again. "What's the matter? Don't you see?"

She laughed, hysterically and soundlessly. I thought she was out of her mind. I almost slapped her to bring her back to her senses but I didn't have to. The noiseless laughter stopped as suddenly as it had started.

"The money," she said simply.

I looked at her.

"In the room," she said. "The money's in the room. If we just turn and leave what in the name of God do we do about the money?"

It was a good question. A hell of a good question. It almost knocked me on my ear.

I'd completely forgotten the money, but now that she reminded me I couldn't think of anything else. Fifty grand in nice green twenty dollar bills reposed in a black satchel in her room and they were staked out around it like expectant vultures.

It was too much.

Then I answered the question. "You get a cab, Cindy. Go to a hotel, stay there. They don't know me. As far as they're concerned you're all by yourself. I'll slip into the apartment and get the money and meet you."

She shook her head. "They have the place surrounded," she said. "Back and front. I'm sure of it."

"So?"

"They'll see you coming out. They're probably in the room right now. Maybe they already have the money. Great God above."

I thought, then shook my head. "No," I said. "Then they wouldn't be sticking around. My guess is that they know where you are but don't know the apartment, maybe not even the building. Is there a back entrance to your place?"

She shook her head.

"A window," I said. "A window in the back that I can get through."

"Locked."

"I'll break it. Where's the satchel? Is it there in the room?"

"Under the bed."

"I'll get it and go out the way I came in. Look, you walk back to Broadway and hail the first cab you see. Get him to drive you to Grand Central, then switch cabs and go to the Sheraton-McAlpin on Broadway and 34th. It's a convention hotel and Reed's type of people won't be likely to be there. Get a double, pay in advance because you don't have luggage. Register as Mr. and Mrs. Ronald Stone and tell 'em I'll be along later."

She repeated the instructions and nodded. She looked as empty-eyed as a sleepwalker. I could only hope that she'd remember what I'd told her, that she wouldn't panic and ruin everything.

"We'll catch a plane first thing in the morning," I added. "One night in the hotel and then we'll be out of this town for good, with no trail behind us. Good enough?"

She hesitated.

I knew what was on her mind.

"You're thinking I could cross you," I said. "You're thinking how easy it would be for me to disappear with the money and leave you high and dry. Right?"

She flushed.

"You'll just have to trust me," I said. "Or else figure out a better way."

She couldn't figure out a better way so she decided to trust me. I gave her twenty for the cab and the room and stood where I was until I saw her catch a cab at the corner of Broadway. Then I lit a cigarette and smoked it all the way down, then dropped it to the sidewalk and squashed it to shreds.

I was ready.

I went back to Amsterdam and walked down to 72nd Street, then headed east until I was opposite her building, or as close to it as I could tell. If I was in luck there would be a driveway I could take.

I was not in luck. The buildings presented a united front and there was no passageway to the rear of her building. I swore softly and tried to think.

Then I got lucky. One of the buildings was a huge apartment building complete with a doorman. I nodded to the doorman and walked inside. He let me go, proving that doormen are as necessary as they are useful, which is to say not at all.

With luck there would be a rear exit from the building's lobby.

I looked for it and found it. I opened the door slowly and stared at the back of the building where Cindy lived and my heart soared. Then I stared some more and my heart sank like a stone.

I saw her window, the one I could drop through to her apartment.

I also saw the mug.

He was small but he looked wiry. He was wearing a grey sharkskin suit with peaked lapels and there was a bulge inside the jacket that meant one of two things. Either he had a breast or he was carrying a gun.

This was a complication.

I tried to figure what my chances might be of taking him and decided they were infinitesimal. Even without the gun he'd be a good bet to set me on my ear. With the gun I was finished. All I had to do was walk out from the doorway and I was as dead as a lox.

I thought for a few seconds about just how pleasant it would not be to be dead. The notion of spending a few hours bleeding on the sidewalk, a few days in a morgue on a cold grey slab, and a few eternities in a hole on Riker's Island was most unappetizing.

So?

Another possibility came to mind. I could turn around, walk back through the lobby, mumble absurd pleasantries to the silly doorman and be on my way. I wasn't in too deep to do that. It would be a cinch.

A cinch. I could say a fond good-bye to Cinderella Sims, another fond good-bye to fifty grand, and that would be that. What the hell, it was better than saying a fond good-bye to life, wasn't it?

Well, wasn't it?

I wasn't so sure about that. I thought about fifty thousand dollars, which was one hell of a lot of dough. I thought about Cinderella Sims, which was one hell of a lot of woman. I thought about the town in Arizona and the newspaper and the family and all sorts of things.

I thought about how empty life had been for a while there, and how empty it would be without the money and the girl.

I thought about that a long time.

And then I thought about something else, something fairly obvious to anybody with half a brain in his head. The monkey in the sharkskin suit didn't know who I was. He didn't even know I existed. And this gave me a hell of a fine edge on him.

Lawrence Block

If I tried to sneak up on him I was dead. If I tried to rush him I was dead. But suppose I came on openly?

I decided it just might work.

I stuck an unlit cigarette in the corner of my mouth and gave the door a heave. It flew open and I went through it and the guy turned around with a look of panic on his face.

"Hey," I called. "Hey, Mac!"

He looked at me.

I walked over to him, talking as I went. "Can't find a light in the whole damned building," I complained. "You got a match on you?"

He pulled out a lighter, still not talking. He flicked it and I leaned toward him to accept the light.

Then I grabbed him.

My thumb and forefinger took him by the throat and he couldn't make a sound. Then I gave him the right to the stomach, throwing it low for luck.

He doubled over.

I let go of his throat and cupped his head with both hands. He was on his way down so I gave him a hand. Two hands.

I brought up a knee and broke his face over it.

I had to let him down slow so he wouldn't make a noise. Then I rolled him over and looked at him. He was a mess. There were a batch of teeth missing from his mouth and his nose was so broken you couldn't tell where it had come from. I had to check his pulse to make sure he was alive, not that I really cared about him.

I used his shirt to cover the pane of glass, then knocked it in with the butt of his revolver. The glass all fell inside the apartment and the noise didn't carry.

I followed on the glass, landed on my feet and looked for the bed. It was a big one and I momentarily regretted that I wouldn't have the pleasure of bouncing around on it with Cindy. But there wasn't time to worry about that sort of thing. It was only a question of time before one of the monkey's pals came around to check on him and I had to work pretty damned fast.

I found the satchel and discovered that fifty grand in twenties is heavy. But I managed to get out with it, climbing up on a chair and then out through the window. From there on it was a cinch.

I kicked the monkey in the face on the way out for luck, then stuck his gun back in his holster. He might need it when he tried to explain things to the rest of them. Then I went right back the way I'd come, straight through the lobby and past the doorman and out onto 72nd Street. There was a cab at the curb and I hopped into the back seat and told him to go to the Sheraton-McAlpin. He went, and I sat there trying to relax.

I had the money. If I wanted to I could ditch Cindy and forget her forever. She'd never find me, not in a million years.

But I couldn't.

I needed her as much as I needed the money. I couldn't settle for half the dream. It had to be all or nothing, the money and Cindy or the hell with the whole shooting match. So I sat back and pretended to relax and the cab finally managed to get to the McAlpin.

I found out which room we were staying in and I went to her.

6

She wasn't just surprised to see me. She was totally astounded. Her eyes went round as saucers, then darted from me to the satchel and back and forth. They had love in them, but I wasn't sure whether the love was for me or for the money.

I didn't care.

"I don't believe it," she said. "You did it. You actually did it!"

I tossed her the satchel. She unzipped the zipper and upended the bag over the bed. Money spilled out of it, neat stacks of twenty dollar notes with cute little rubber bands around them.

"Look at it," she said reverently. "Fifty thousand dollars. Did you ever see that much money before?"

Once, when I was a little kid about to graduate from grammar school, they took the lot of us to Washington to look around and admire the miracle of democratic government. The package deal included a visit to the bureau of engraving and printing, and in the course of a half hour I saw well over a million dollars. But I didn't have the heart to tell her about it.

Besides, this was different. The dough at the bureau was not my money. This was.

"Tell me how you did it," she said. "Oh, I knew I was doing the right thing when I told you about it. You saved everything, Ted. Tell me how you did it. Tell me everything."

I told her everything, omitting only the occasional temptations to forget the whole thing that had crossed my mind in weak moments. Her eyes shone all the way through and there was a special gleam in them when I told how I'd made a mess out of the monkey's face. The recounting of the fight, one-sided as it was, seemed to give her a special charge.

When I had brought the yarn up to date I relaxed and took her in my arms. But she didn't relax. I could sense the wheels going around inside that pretty head. And I wondered if her mind ever slept.

"Bunkie Craig," she said.

I looked at her, questioningly.

"The one you pushed around. That's who it must have been. The others wouldn't carry a gun, but he'd be naked without one. And the description fits. It must have been him."

Naturally the name meant nothing, but it was comforting to know that the gorilla wasn't some innocent bystander. I nodded.

"You should have killed him."

My eyebrows went up. "What's the matter? Did you hate him that much?"

"I hated him, but that's neither here nor there. You should have killed him."

"Why?"

"He saw you," she explained patiently. "Before they didn't know who you were, didn't realize there was anybody helping me. Now they know. If you had killed him he wouldn't be able to finger you."

"Dead men tell no tales?"

"Something like that."

I shrugged it off. "He won't tell any tales for awhile, Cindy. He'll be in the hospital first."

"But not forever. Maybe it won't make a difference, but I wish you'd finished him permanently. I hate to take chances."

I tried to shrug it off again but I didn't quite make it. I was getting a new picture of her now, a picture with a lot less of the softness and gentleness; a picture of a woman who could be as cold and calculating as an adding machine. I suppose it should have scared me. Somehow it didn't.

"We'll get a good night's sleep now," I said optimistically. It was after four and there didn't seem to be too much chance of our getting a night's sleep. A morning's sleep, perhaps. But there wasn't much left of the night.

"Then we catch a plane in the morning to Phoenix. I'll buy a car there and we'll head for a small town, pick up a copy of *Editor & Publisher* and look at the newspaper listings. From there on it's a cinch."

"My clothes are in my room."

"You'll buy new ones in Phoenix."

"I can't go on the plane like this."

"Neither can I," I said. "I need a jacket and a tie at the very least. And you need something a little more formal than dungarees and a shirt of mine. But for fifty grand I can stand a few hours of mild embarrassment. So can you."

She lowered her eyes. "I'm sorry," she said. "Of course I can. I wasn't thinking."

"We'll take a hack to Idlewild," I went on. "We'll check first on the phone, catch the time so that we don't have to sit around the waiting room. We might be spotted. It's not worth the chance."

"Right."

"Once we're in Phoenix we'll be clear. As long as we're in New York we've got to be on guard. I'll be glad to get out of here."

She nodded, agreeing.

There wasn't anything more to say. I reached for her and hauled her down on the bed, pulling her close to me. Her body was warm and her eyes very beautiful. She looked very tired but I didn't let that stop me.

I was tired myself. The fun and games with Bunkie Craig had hardly been designed to relax a person. On top of that I'd had more in the way of horizontal harmony in the past twenty-four hours than most men have in a month.

Still, I needed her. I was tense and my nerves were strung tight and fine as piano wire. I had to relax and I needed the relaxation she could bring me.

I unbuttoned her shirt. I played with her breasts until her nipples saluted me.

I took off her pants.

I found other things to do with her.

"Ted —"

"I was a good boy, Cindy. I beat up the bad guy and got the money and brought it straight to you. Wasn't I a good boy?"

"You were a very good boy."

"And a good boy deserves a reward, doesn't he?"

"Of course."

"Do I get my reward, Cindy?"

I got my reward.

Her hips heaved me to heaven and her mouth drained my mouth and her breasts were softer than snow. She made everything worthwhile — the risks, the flight, the whole thing. I had earned my half of the fifty grand when I got the satchel from her apartment. Now she was earning her half flat on her back in a big double bed in room 53 of the Sheraton-McAlpin, earning it very well.

It began, it endured, it ended.

I slept.

She woke up before I did. I felt her lips on mine and I opened my eyes. I reached for her and she jumped away, a pixieish smile on her face.

She looked good in the morning.

"Rise and shine," she said. "We've got a plane to catch."

I tried to put my eyes into focus. It didn't work. I sat up in bed and stared at the wall.

"What time is it? I better get dressed and call the airport."

"I called them already."

"From here?"

She nodded and I swore under my breath. "You should have called from a pay phone," I said. "They can trace it this way. If the switchboard operator is in on it —"

"Don't be ridiculous," she said. "You know what the odds against that are?"

I knew. I still didn't like it.

"When does the plane leave?"

"Three-thirty."

I calculated rapidly. "Call Room Service," I said. "Have them send up some ham and eggs and a pot of coffee. Then we'll sit around here until a quarter past two. That way we'll get to Idlewild just in time."

"I already did," she said. "I hope you like your eggs scrambled."

The food came and we ate it, then sat around until it was time to go. I settled with the hotel, grabbed a cab for the airport. It was silly, but I was tense as a wire on the way. The weather was good and the ride was pleasant but I couldn't relax.

"Did you reserve tickets for us?"

She nodded.

"What name?"

"Mr. and Mrs. Ronald Stone. Same name as we used at the hotel."

I got mad at her. "That was pretty stupid. If they trace us to the hotel they'll be able to trace us to Phoenix. That wasn't too bright, Cindy."

"I had to. The call went through the switchboard. I couldn't use another name."

"That's why you should have called from a pay phone, dammit. Jesus, of all the brilliant moves — "

She looked sick to her stomach and I forced myself to relax. "I'm sorry," I said. "It probably won't make any difference. They'll never even trace us to the hotel."

I tried to sound sure of myself. If I did I was a good actor. Because I was scared.

I picked up the tickets at the TWA desk and paid for them with some of McGuire's twenties, hoping the serial numbers hadn't been recorded anywhere. It didn't seem likely but it gave me something else to worry about. Not that I needed it. There was plenty to worry about as it was.

We waited by the flight gate for the plane to open up for us and I felt about as conspicuous as a whore in church. We weren't exactly dressed for the flight. She was attired cleverly in dungarees and one of my shirts and I didn't look a hell of a lot better. I had on a pair of khakis and a dirty white shirt without a tie. I needed a shave pretty badly — a few more days without one and we could head for Frisco, get a loft on North Beach and pose as beatniks.

And the satchel was much too heavy. I had the eerie feeling that anyone looking at it could tell at a glance that it was loaded with money that didn't belong to us. I wanted to put it in my pocket or something. It really worried me.

They called our flight and we were the first passengers on it. We found seats up front and I let her have the one by the window. I set the satchel in my lap and tried to cover it up with my hands. It didn't work.

The plane filled up. The stewardess welcomed us aboard and said some other silly things, we put out our cigarettes and fastened our safety belts, the flight took off. It was a smooth takeoff and smooth flying all the way. The ham and eggs stayed in my stomach.

The three of us landed at Phoenix — me, Cindy and the fifty grand. The three of us got out of the plane and into a cab. Cindy and I looked like wilted flowers. The money was fresh as a field of daisies.

I checked us in at the De Milo Arms, a slightly better-than-average hotel off Schwerner Square in the middle of downtown Phoenix. Now we were Mr. and Mrs. Gerald Harris. The Ronald Stones had disappeared for good.

The bellboy tried to take the satchel from me but I didn't let him. He led us to our room and I tipped him and he disappeared. When he was gone I locked the door and put the chain on. I pulled down the window shade, then sat down on the edge of the bed and opened the satchel.

The money, miraculously, was still there.

"Look at it," she said. "Just look at it."

She scared me. She sounded like a knight gazing upon the Holy Grail. I wondered just how much she would do for fifty thousand dollars, just how much she had already done. There was something phony about her story of the con game operation, something that didn't quite ring true. I'd been thinking about it on the plane ride but I couldn't quite put my finger on it. I was fairly certain she'd lied somehow about her own part in the proceedings but I wasn't sure how or why.

And I didn't want to think about it.

What did it matter? We were free, clear, safe. We were in Phoenix and no one knew it. We had fifty thousand dollars and the world belonged to us.

She echoed my thoughts. "We're safe, Ted. We're out of New York and no one knows it. We're safe."

I was too exhausted emotionally to say a damn thing.

She stood up. "I'm taking some money and going shopping," she said. "You stay here until I come back. Then you can go out and see about a car, pick up some clothes for yourself, things like that. Okay?"

It was okay with me.

I waited until she was out of the building. I watched through the window and saw her head down the street toward the section where the stores seemed to be.

It was only four-thirty. We'd gotten a break—the time in the plane had been largely offset by the time belts we had crossed on the way. There was still time for her to get some shopping done, maybe even time for me to see about a car after she got back.

Meanwhile I had things to do.

I picked up the phone, called Room Service. I told them to send up a fifth of Jack Daniels and some ice. I signed for the tab, slipped the bellboy a buck and smiled while he thanked me.

The Jack Daniels was silky smooth and I needed it desperately. I made myself a tall cool one and relaxed in an easy chair with it, sipping it slowly and tasting it all the way down.

I had a lot of thinking to do.

With the liquor clearing my head and with Cindy's pleasantly disturbing body out of my way I could concentrate on all the things that were hard to concentrate upon otherwise. The con game was too elaborate to be a lie and her story was a little too rough to be entirely true. I could have ignored it all but something made me go back to it, run it through my mind for a quick check. I knew a little about the standard bunco routines from my police beat days, and I couldn't quite see how an innocent doll like Cindy could have come home with fifty thousand dollars that belonged by all rules to the smoothies who'd conned it out of McGuire in the first place. Con men don't work that way. True, there's a maxim that every con man is by definition a sucker. The big boys in the business don't hold onto much of the money they pick from the marks. But there are several ways of being a sucker, and the idea of Cindy Sims walking off with their take struck me as a little on the silly side.

I told myself to relax and forget it. Suppose she was lying. What earthly difference did it make? I had the money and the girl and that ought to be enough. The money made it fun to be awake and the girl made it fun to go to sleep. To hell with reality.

But something nagged at me. Maybe it was the combination of the liquor that cleared my head and the fact that she wasn't there to muddle me up again. I don't think I could have looked at her and thought about how she must be lying to me. But with her out of the room it was easy.

Did it make a difference? If we split up now it didn't. If I took my twenty-five thou and she took hers it didn't matter at all. I'm not the type to get conscience traumas. For twenty-five grand I can forget a hell of a lot of things, such as the moral aspects of almost anything.

But we weren't going to split, and with the two of us together as man and wife, her role in the episode became very relevant. I knew next to nothing about her, just the superficial trivia that she had seen fit to tell me. The dream I'd been dreaming called for full knowledge of her, full knowledge and full understanding and full love. And my knowledge of her was far from full.

I sipped my drink and thought about her. There were so many points to her story that didn't ring true. According to her, Cinderella Sims was her real name, wished on her by highly imaginative parents. But she had picked another name to work under in Tahoe, Lucille Kraft or something like that.

This made no sense at all. If her name had been, say, Hepzibah Klunk, I could see why she would change it on the job. But why alter something simple like Cindy Sims, something a hell of a lot more euphonious than Lucille Kraft?

It didn't jibe.

Nor did the innocent pose fit with the wish that I had killed Bunkie Craig. Nor did the careful pose fit with the sloppiness of calling the terminal from the hotel room. There were too many inconsistencies and they were sticking out all over the place.

They bothered me. Bothered me a hell of a lot. I wanted to quit thinking about them but I couldn't.

I could check on her, up to a point anyhow. I could get in touch with Tahoe and run both her names through the hotel, could find out if that much of her story was true. But there was no rush. She wasn't going to do anything to me, not now, and she wasn't going to take the money and ditch me. I was fairly sure of that.

I tried to decide whether or not it made sense to stick the dough in the hotel safe for the time being. That would keep her from taking off with it, but it would also let on that I felt something was a bit smelly in the state of Denmark. That phrase, by the way, has always been a source of consternation to me. There's very little that is rotten in the state of Denmark. Denmark has always been one of my favorite countries, and if there was something rotten it was in the state of Arizona.

I mused on that point, drank a little more of the Jack Daniels, then took the elevator to the lobby to see what, if anything, was happening at the local newsstand. They didn't have *Editor & Publisher*. The newsie told me I could get it across the street, that he only carried a small line for people who wanted something to kill time with. I decided that walking all the way across the street took more effort than I felt like dispensing so I went back to the room and waited for Cindy.

She came back looking very beautiful in a sexy black blouse and a pair of white slacks. I don't imagine the white slacks were very practical — one wearing and they'd look as though they'd been slept in — but on her they looked so good that it didn't matter. I talked to her about nothing very important, gave her a quick kiss and went out, hoping that both she and the money would be there when I got back.

I bought a lightweight grey suit, a batch of shirts and some underwear, leaving my clothes for the department store to donate to charity or something. Probably to burn, because they certainly weren't good for much else any more. Then I picked up a copy of *E & P,* breezed through the listings while I downed a cup of coffee and a toasted English, checked a few ads that looked like better-than-average possibilities and headed back to the hotel.

She was there and so was the money. She told me how good I looked and I told her again how good she looked and we necked for awhile, stopping before we got too caught up in what we were doing to take time out for dinner.

Dinner was a pair of blood-rare steaks in the best restaurant in town, juicy red meat with baked potatoes and a drink before and Irish coffee after. Dinner made a big difference — I felt so completely at peace with the world that I didn't care whether or not the money was there when we got back to the room.

It was. We looked at it, smiled, shoved it under the bed and got undressed. There was something strange about making tender love on top of fifty thousand in nice green twenty dollar bills, but we got used to it. It wasn't too hard.

In fact, after not too long we forgot all about those nice green twenty dollar bills. We got sort of carried away with what we were doing, and the room turned upside down, and the lights went out and on and out and on again, and my heart started punching holes in my chest, and...well, you get the general idea.

Afterwards I put my face between her warm breasts and inhaled the fragrance of her until sleep came. It's a pleasant way to go to sleep.

Very pleasant.

Which was a fortunate thing, because the next day was not.

After breakfast the next morning I made what I thought was an eminently reasonable suggestion. I told her I was going to take the money and deposit it in a Phoenix bank. It made good sense. That way there was no chance of it getting lost or stolen. We didn't have to watch it like hawks.

Moreover, it gave us an aura of respectability that cash would not give us. Money in the bank is a lot more solid in appearance than money in a wallet or a black leather satchel. It would give us a foothold on the problem of establishing credit. Imagine walking into a newspaper broker with a bagful of twenties, for Christ's sake. That would be one for the books.

And, of course, there was another unspoken point involved. If the dough was in a joint account, neither of us could steal it from the other. I didn't mention this and neither did she, but naturally we both thought of it instantly.

She wouldn't hear of it.

"We have to have it in cash," she said.

I asked why.

"Suppose we have to run. Suppose they get onto us and we have to leave town."

"How?"

"It could happen."

I didn't know how in the world it could but I let it pass. I told her that you didn't have to be in town to keep an account open, that checks on the account would clear in any bank in the country, that Reed and his rover boys could hardly take the dough away from us if we kept it in the bank.

She still wouldn't hear of it.

A bell rang somewhere in my head and I let it drop. I pretended to agree with her, told her we might need it in a hurry and that she was one hundred percent right. I hoped she'd believe me, that she wouldn't think I was suspicious.

I was very suspicious.

I made up some story that I can't remember, something about going out to see a newspaper broker to see what was available that wasn't listed in *E & P*. Once I got away from her my hands started to shake. Something was wrong, very wrong. I didn't know what it was and I sure as hell wanted to find out.

There were two possibilities and either or both of them could be the answer. One was that she was planning on ditching me as soon as she felt secure, that she wanted the cash around so she could take it along. But I couldn't quite swallow it—she was as secure as she would ever be right now. She had had plenty of chances to ditch me while I was buying my suit the day before.

There was another possibility. Something could be funny about the money. It could be hot, with the serial numbers listed. In that case it could be spent a little at a time but not in quantity. If we stuck the lot of it in a bank we were through.

Or it could be counterfeit.

That seemed impossible. I took a twenty from my wallet and looked it over. It looked just like every other twenty I'd ever seen in my life, but of course I was no judge of twenties. If it was a phony it was one hell of a good one. I could even see the red and blue threads in the paper, the ones that counterfeiters aren't supposed to be able to duplicate.

I wondered.

If it was counterfeit, it sure as hell figured that she wouldn't want me depositing a load of it in a bank. We'd be in the jug in a minute. But if it was counterfeit that knocked the props out from under her whole story. No mark could unload fifty grand worth of schlock on a con ring. No mark would have access to counterfeit dough.

Counterfeit. Queer, schlock, funny money.

Was it possible?

And if it was, how in hell could I check it without getting nailed for trying to pass it?

The first thing to do was run the Tahoe story through the mill. If that checked I could forget the rest and save myself some headaches. If it didn't, I could worry about it later.

I put in a person-to-person call to the manager of West of the Lake in Tahoe, knowing that I'd get straight dope from him. I'd never heard of that particular club but it was a dollars-to-doughnuts cinch that it, like every other club in Nevada, was syndicate property. And syndicate people in legit business are the best damned businessmen in the world. You'll never find a crooked roulette wheel in a Nevada house, or a fast-fingered stickman, or a slippery dealer. They play things straight as can be. The house percentage is enough.

The manager was a man named Rogers. He was very obliging and most willing to check on the two prospective employees who had given his name as a reference. If they had ever worked there he would let me know about it.

No, he said, he had never employed a Lucille Kraft. No, he also said, he had never employed a Cinderella Sims either.

As a matter of fact, he added, he used only men as cashiers. Hadn't had a girl in a cashier's cage in, well, five years at the very least.

I managed to thank him before I dropped the receiver on the hook and sat down, my head spinning and my mind going around in very strange circles.

Next I had to check the dough.

It was a gamble but I had to take it. I found the best way to do it, the simple approach. I walked into the first bank I came to, found the assistant manager and told him I'd picked up a twenty in Detroit and I wanted to know whether it was good or not. "Something funny-looking about it," I told him. "I wouldn't want to pass it off to anybody and have them get stuck with it."

It sounded like just the sort of thing a solid citizen might say.

He took it, studied it and snapped it a couple times. "You wait right here, Mr. Cannon," he told me. "I want to have a look at it under the glass. It looks okay but you never know for sure unless you look real close."

He disappeared with it and I wanted to turn and run. I'd given him a phony name and a phony story, and if he was calling the cops I was through for sure. But if I ran now I was dead no matter what happened. I forced myself to wait, lit a cigarette and pretended to be calm.

He was back in a minute.

"You got one hell of a fine eye," he told me.

"Counterfeit?"

"It sure is. Wouldn't have spotted it myself, to tell you the truth. See here around the seal?"

I looked where he was pointing.

"Little different than it's supposed to be. You got another twenty on you for comparison?"

I told him no. I did, but it was just as phony as the one in his hand. Just as phony as the whole fifty thousand bucks' worth.

"Don't suppose it matters. It is a wrong one, though. And a real pretty job."

I thanked him very thoroughly and got up to go. It was about that time that I realized he still had my twenty. That was all I needed. I had to get it back.

I was nonchalant.

"Say," I said, "you wouldn't mind if I took that bill for a souvenir, would you? I mean, I certainly wouldn't try to pass it or anything. I'd sort of like to keep it as a reminder of how I got stuck for twenty bucks."

He hesitated. I kept my mouth shut. If I sold him too hard he might tumble.

He sighed. "We're supposed to report any counterfeit to the police," he said, and my heart sank. That was all I needed. "Then they send the bill to Washington, check you out to make sure you're okay just as a matter of form, and I don't know what all. I suspect they have a special ceremonial burning of the bill in the Justice Department."

He laughed. I tried to chuckle along with him.

"You say you picked this up in Detroit?"

I nodded weakly.

He thought some more, then shrugged. "Tell you the truth, I'm damned if I can see what good it'll do to bother the police. Just waste their time, and yours and mine as well. Why don't you just take this along with you and forget you ever showed it to me?"

I could have kissed him. I thanked him again, returned the bill to my wallet and strolled out of the bank. My knees were knocking together and I thought I was going to fall apart at the seams. I needed a drink badly, and that wasn't all I needed.

I needed an explanation.

7

There was a ten, a five and two singles in my wallet along with the nest of phony twenties. It was a good thing — otherwise I would have gone thirsty. Until then I'd been passing the stuff all over town like a drunken sailor, but now that I knew what it was it wasn't the same at all. The money was burning a hole in my pocket, all right, but it was different. Now I just wanted to be rid of it.

I found a back booth in a dark bar on a side street and settled myself down to a double bourbon with water on the side. I swallowed the bourbon and looked at the water. It looked back at me.

Things were moving too fast, much too fast. I looked for the little lever in my head that would let me turn my mind back and start over.

I found it.

A girl whose name was undoubtedly neither Lucille Kraft nor Cinderella Sims had fifty thousand dollars' worth of counterfeit twenties that didn't belong to her. The people who had originally owned them were chasing her. And she was running, but where?

The thing to do, I told myself, was to examine the situation through Cindy's mind. This was easier said than done. I just couldn't manage to think the way she probably thought. For a while I sat around feeling sorry over this little incapacity of mine. Then I felt glad about it. My projection may have been limited, but perhaps it was better to be able to think rationally than to be able to think like Cindy Sims.

So I did something else. I tried putting myself in her place. What would I have done?

Putting myself in her place wasn't that easy itself. I just didn't know too much about her, didn't know who she was or what she had done. Most of what I did know was negative information — she hadn't worked with a con mob, hadn't held a cashier's job at a club in Tahoe, didn't have fifty grand all of a sudden, and, of course, did not make it a practice to tell the truth come hell or high water.

The positive information told me that she had stolen a pile from a gang of counterfeiters. But what in hell she was trying to do with it was, for the moment, beyond me.

Why steal it in the first place?

Well, it had to be worth something. If not, counterfeiters wouldn't take the trouble to print it up. I tried to remember what we'd run into in Louisville that might fit into things; I couldn't come up with too much, but I got a few little glimmers.

A counterfeiting ring, as well as I remembered, was a model for an extremely loose organization that worked with extreme efficiency. At the very top there was a small group of men who were the financial kingpins. Either they included an engraver and printer in their number or they managed to contract for the production through their own private sources.

The men at the top were completely autonomous. They didn't hire anybody. They handled two facets only — production and distribution. They never passed anything themselves. Instead they sold their product to roving mobs of bill-passers who went from one big town to the next, changing as much of the dough as they could.

The mobs themselves were organized in similar fashion, with a small combine arranging for the original purchase and selling small quantities to smaller men. At the very bottom there was the tiny small-time crook who bought a hundred dollars' worth of queer at a time for ten to twenty dollars and worked it into circulation by himself, making purchases as small as he dared and keeping the change.

It was like any operation where the illegal aspect consisted of a product. Like the narcotics trade, for example, or like bootlegging. But there was an important difference.

There were risks in dope pushing. And in bootlegging.

In counterfeiting the risks were almost nonexistent.

I sipped more water, waggled a finger at the waiter and downed the refill in a hurry. It was beginning to come back to me. The picture was soaking in.

Where was I? Yes—the risks, and how there weren't any. You see, in both dope and alcohol the product itself presented some overwhelming problems. If you wanted to supply dope on a large scale you had to produce it from the raw opium, which in this country is quite impossible, or bring it in from overseas. Your agents can get arrested going through customs. Your shipments can be seized in huge quantities and destroyed. And simple possession of any quantity whatsoever of the stuff is enough to land you in jail.

Bootlegging is similar. Here you have to produce the stuff, have to distill it, and a distillation operation has to leave some clues lying around. You have to buy supplies in quantity. You have to have a good-sized plant in order to make a good-sized amount of the stuff. As a result, you automatically leave yourself open for possible arrest.

But counterfeiting is something else entirely.

Production presents no problems. Your "factory" consists of a set of plates, a little flat-bed or rotary press weighing maybe fifteen pounds at most, and a quantity of plain white paper to print on. Everything you need fits into a suitcase.

The distribution picture is even more attractive. It's not against the law for a citizen to possess a counterfeit bill if he doesn't know it's counterfeit. Otherwise a guy like me could have been arrested in the Merchants' Bank of Phoenix. The law has to prove knowledge on the criminal's part. And this isn't easy to do.

Possession of a quantity of identical counterfeit bills, is, of course, grounds for conviction. Possession of a counterfeit bill by a man already arrested for counterfeiting is also grounds for conviction, often enough.

But the nature of the business is such that an individual without a criminal record can pass a bill at any time with total impunity. Counterfeit? Gee, officer, I didn't know it was counterfeit. I mean, somebody must of stuck me with it. I never look too close, I don't know, maybe I ought to. But officer, I didn't do anything...

People get caught. The mobs who get nailed good and hard are the hit-and-run mobs that the big boys supply. They run the risks because they're in town while the phony stuff is turning up.

But the boys remain untouchable. If things ever get hot they stick the plates in a safe deposit box and let a bank watch it for them. Once every few years somebody somewhere gets a tip and catches a big fish or two with a load of schlock in their apartment. But it just doesn't happen too often.

I finished my drink. The stuff that was going through my mind was old stuff, a basic review of the fundamental principles of counterfeiting. It was fun, but it wasn't explaining the Sinful Saga of Cindy Sims.

But I was beginning to get a glimmer.

Suppose I'd stolen fifty thousand dollars' worth of schlock from a nestful of big boys. It was worth stealing, of course. It was worth in the neighborhood of, say, five to ten grand on the not-very-open market. My banker had practically gone into orbit over the quality of this particular schlock, so in this case it was probably worth ten, maybe even more.

If your name is Rockefeller, ten grand is nothing to get sweaty about. But if your name is Sims, or Lindsay for that matter, it is. Ten grand is ten grand, and while it is not fifty grand, it is not hay either.

So it was worth stealing.

But what in hell did you do with it once you stole it?

Well, that was easy. You found somebody who was willing to pay ten grand for it, and then you sold it to him, or them, or whoever it was. You sure as hell didn't try to pass it all yourself. That would quite possibly take you several lifetimes, and before long some cop would grab you, and the ball game would be thoroughly over. Besides, why not get the whole pie at once?

And then the whole thing hit me. It was so goddamned funny I laughed out loud.

Here was Cindy. Sleeping with Reed, or whoever he was, and hating him and hungry for his money. So she bundled fifty grand in schlock into a little black satchel and took off with it.

Now who in the name of God was she going to sell it to?

Not a hit-and-run mob, because she simply didn't *know* a hit-and-run mob. Not a rival outfit, because she simply didn't *know* a rival outfit. She was a cipher, a little person who just happened to fall amongst thieves — in this case counterfeiters.

And the only people she knew with any use for the dough were the ones she'd stolen it from.

It was funny. It was very funny, and it was certainly worth laughing over. It was also very sad and worth crying over but I somehow didn't feel like crying. I was having too much fun.

Cindy had the money, all right. And she could sell it to Reed — but Reed would hardly be a willing customer. He probably had an overwhelming desire to twist her pretty neck. She couldn't walk right up to him and say: Here's the money, now pay me. If she did he'd do the very natural thing — he'd kill her.

She had to run away from him.

But the further she ran the less her money was worth. Reed was her only customer. He was the man she had to do business with and the man she had to steer clear of, and the end product of a relationship like this could only be frustration.

I saw it all now — anyway, most of it. She grabbed the bundle and ran to New York. Then she saw which end was up and wired Reed or something to let him know approximately where she was. Not precisely where, because she was scared stiff.

Then she waited for him, hoping two things — that he would find her, and that he would not find her.

Uh-huh.

So she waited, scared spitless, until he showed. Then he showed and she took one look at him and got out of town.

Now, by all rules, she was waiting for him to show up again.

It all meshed. Now for the first time my part in the deal was beginning to make sense. She'd managed to blunder into me, probably the way she said — saw me watching her and figured me for one of Reed's men.

Then she must have decided she could use me.

Two people could do it. One to make contact and the other to hold back with the money. That way there wouldn't be any killing. I'd handle the changes while she stayed in the shadows, and then we would split.

Except, obviously, we wouldn't split. If we were going to split she wouldn't have fed me a story on a silver spoon. She'd have leveled with me and we would have been planning the bit together all along. She must have figured that, while ten grand might have been worth all the aggravation she'd gone through, five grand certainly wasn't. She wanted the whole pie.

Everything made sense — the lies, the stupidity of her phone calls from the hotel, leaving her a convenient out when Reed showed up. Her cheap apartment and her pinchpenny ways until we'd gotten together. Sure — she was scared stiff to pass any of the dough by herself. So was I, now that I knew what it was. It must have been a break for her when I started spending her dough as if it was real, giving her a chance to live like a human being again.

It all added up. If you thought of it as a carefully planned crime you could look at it forever without getting the picture. That was the whole thing—it had been about as carefully planned as an airplane crash. Her appalling stupidity from the beginning to end was the key to the whole mess.

I wondered how she was going to arrange the deal without filling me in. She probably didn't know any more than I did. The way I figured it, she was playing it by ear the way she'd played it all up to now, hoping that something would break right for her.

If I hadn't tumbled we'd probably run from Phoenix to Miami, from Miami to Philly, from Philly to Cleveland. Somewhere along the line we'd be arrested because I'd be passing too many bills at once since I didn't know there was anything wrong with them.

Or, somewhere along the line Reed would catch up with us.

And kill us.

And on that sobering thought I had another drink.

One thing didn't add up, and that was Reed's angle in the gambit. I could see him hating her for crossing him, and I could see him hating her enough to chase her and kill her, but I could not see him dragging a small army of professionals along with him. That I could not see at all. He might be ready and willing to run all over the world for a crack at her, but the rest of them couldn't. She was good in the hay but not good enough to sleep with all of them, for Christ's sake.

Reed figured to forget it. Forgetting ten grand sounds like forgetting that white cow again, but when all you have to do is print up a fresh batch it's not quite so hard to take. Revenge wasn't enough of a motive and neither was the desire to recoup a relatively minor investment. What could it have cost him in terms of time and paper? Not a hell of a lot. I've seen the presses at the *Times* roll off a few hundred impressions a minute. It's an impressive sight. Granted, a hand press is slower. But not slow enough.

He was spending more money dragging his forces all over the continent than the fifty grand cost him in the first place.

So why was he wasting his time?

I wanted a close look at the schlock. I wasn't quite courageous enough to stare at it in the middle of the bar, or even in a booth in the back of the bar, so I retreated to the relative privacy of the men's room. There were two types of cans—the ones with doors and the ones without. The ones with the doors cost ten cents, and I normally wasn't buggy enough about privacy to squander a dime.

Privacy was suddenly worth ten cents.

I locked the door with me inside it and sat down. It feels pretty silly to sit on a toilet without having anything to do but you can get used to it. When I was used to it I got out my wallet and hauled out a twenty.

It looked perfectly real to me.

I held it up to the light and studied it. Whoever had engraved it was a genius. Most counterfeits—and I've seen a few bills at Louisville headquarters—are horribly bad. It just doesn't have to be good. People simply do not know what money looks like.

Think I'm kidding? I hope you do, because I am about to give you a little exhibition.

Take a one dollar bill. You've probably seen and handled and received and spent more of that denomination than any other. Let's work on the front first, or the obverse side, as it's properly called.

Which way is Washington facing? What does it say, letter for letter, under his picture? Who are the two people who sign the bill, and which side does each of them sign on? How many times does the word "one" appear on the face of the bill?

Now the reverse, which is tougher. There are two circles, showing the front and back of the seal of the United States. Which is which? What are two Latin phrases on the reverse of the Great Seal? There's a number on the reverse of the bill that appears nowhere else on it. Ever notice it? Where is it?

That gives you the simplest of ideas. When you take into consideration the fact that people who make change look at a bill only long enough to see what denomination it is, you get a little more of the picture.

See?

I looked some more at the twenty, wishing I had a real one to compare it with. I didn't, but even without it I knew the hunk of paper I was holding in my hand was an incredible job. Almost too good to be true, and there's no pun intended there. As far as the engraving itself went, it was just about impossible to tell it from straight stuff. There were undoubtedly little dissimilarities that a professional would see, like the bit with the seal. But I was looking at the seal and I couldn't see a thing wrong with it. I was fairly certain no cashier could either.

But I knew what made the difference. Same thing that always made the difference.

The paper.

I held the bill with a hand on each end and snapped it. The paper was good and strong and it felt like real money. That was the first step right there.

I held it to the light and saw that they'd done it up brown. I could see the little threads in the paper, the wisps of red and blue that identify real American money and make our dough the toughest in the world to duplicate. The counterfeiters had taken the time to paint the little lines in. It's a hell of a job, not always worth it. Only the top stuff ever has it.

Only...

Something was wrong. I shook my head angrily, knowing something was wrong and that there was something I wasn't remembering properly. Something I'd read, or heard, or learned, and something I was forgetting.

Lines in the paper...

I remembered. The big boys never bothered with the lines. It was a hard job and they didn't bother with it. The hit-and-run mobs painted the lines or didn't paint the lines at their own discretion.

Which meant that Reed and his boys didn't produce it. They were just a hit-and-run mob, a group of rover boys who worked a town at a time and spread the stuff around.

That didn't make any sense either.

Because if they were a hit-and-run mob they wouldn't be chasing all over hell to get back the dough Cindy had stolen from them. They wouldn't have the time or the resources.

It didn't make any sense at all.

Why had they painted the lines in? Maybe they were bigger than I thought, or maybe I was a little shakier than I realized on the details of the noble profession of counterfeiting. They could be a big combination, eliminating middle men and supplying stuff straight to pushers. Or they could be a hit-and-run mob with their own plates and a slightly tremendous organization.

It was too much to think about.

I looked at the piece of queer in my hand and found one of the pretty red lines. A good job. It looked just like part of the paper, which of course was what it was supposed to look like.

I licked the tip of my finger and rubbed it off.

It was still there.

A hell of a good job, I admitted. The ink didn't rub off. They had done this up brown, all right.

I used my fingernail to scrape off the surface of the paper.

And stared at the line. And gaped.

The line was still there. The goddamned lines were part of the goddamned paper.

Just like the government made them.

There was a bad moment. To be completely honest, there were quite a few bad moments. I rubbed and rubbed at the hunk of schlock in my hand and wondered whether or not I was sane. It was relatively difficult to tell.

I figured it out gingerly. Slowly, gradually, things began to make their own kind of sense. I remembered something that I read somewhere and thought about it, rubbing the counterfeit bill like Aladdin with that lamp of his.

Once upon a time—I think it was around the turn of the century, but I could be a hundred years away—there was a man whose name I have blissfully forgotten. He was a counterfeiter, a loner who somehow never wound up behind bars. The cops knew he was a counterfeiter, all right. They knew what bills he had made. They occasionally grabbed his passing phonies.

There was only one catch. They couldn't prove his bills were counterfeit in a court of law. He was too good. A defense lawyer could have a lot of fun handling him, challenging the prosecutor to tell the difference between the alleged schlock and the real thing.

Seems there was no difference.

To begin with, the guy engraved a perfect set of plates, which is no mean accomplishment. But that's only half of it. The guy also perfected a method of getting paper that counterfeiters have always dreamed of doing, laying awake nights as they hatched their fiendish plots. None of them managed, none but this one particular guy. God knows how he did it, but what he did was slightly magnificent.

He took a one-dollar bill, you see, and he bleached it. Bleached it dead fish-belly white.

Then he printed a ten on it.

Get the picture? Here you have these perfect plates, and these perfect inks, and now you use the government's own paper to print on. The result is as good as Washington can do. And this little guy, may his soul rest in peace, was the only man in history who figured out how to do it.

Up until now.

Now Reed and his charming chiselers had doped out that same little process. That was why their paper happened to be perfect—it happened to be government paper. That'll do it.

They'd printed up a satchel full of the stuff, with some small error on their plates, and they had permitted a chiseling charmer named, as far as I knew, Cinderella Sims, to carry it off.

I could see why they wanted it back.

What I couldn't see, not entirely, was what in the name of God above Cindy and I were going to do with it. Sell it back to Reed? Oh, sure. Just like that. Pass it? There were easier ways to make a few thousand dollars, ways that didn't carry the risk of a stretch in a cell. Skip the country with it? The hell with that. I like America. I'm happier here than I'd be in, say, Afghanistan. Or Turkey. Or Outer Mongolia.

Besides, why in hell should I skip the country? All I had done was pass a couple of phonies that nobody had to know about, beaten up a hood, transported a woman across state lines for decidedly immoral purposes. Cindy seemed unlikely to turn me in as a Mann Act violator, the hood seemed unlikely to press charges, and no one was going to hit me with anything for passing the counterfeit bills.

So I was clear. All I had to do was throw away the few bills I had left, get out of Phoenix in a hurry, put Cindy Sims far from my mind, and live the good clean life of a solid citizen. It wasn't a hard thing to do. I was throwing away money that I could never spend anyway and I was taking a shot at a much saner way of life.

Suddenly I felt very good.

Suddenly I also felt pretty ridiculous sitting there on the pot. I got up, having an insane wish to do something with the counterfeit other than what its manufacturer had intended, restrained myself mightily, and sauntered out of the men's room. There was still time for a drink and I had one at my table.

"Why don't you buy one for me?"

She was blonde and busty and an argument against celibacy. She had a strong face with high cheekbones and large blue eyes and a red mouth that was a positive sex symbol. Her lips were parted slightly and sex spilled out between them. Come to think of it, why *didn't* I buy her a drink?

So I did. She ordered a daiquiri and put it away in record time. She told me her name was Rhonda King, which I doubted, and I told her my name was Nat Crowley, which was also pretty doubtful, all in all. Her feet played games with my feet and her eyes turned into little blue lodestones, drawing me into them. She was quite an experience, let me tell you.

"This bar is noisy, Nat. Couldn't we go somewhere else? Someplace quiet?"

I felt obscure tugs of loyalty to Sensuous Cindy, then gave them up. What the hell, I was leaving Cindy, wasn't I? Besides, she was the little bitch who was dragging me down Nightmare Alley without telling me what the nightmare was all about. I didn't owe Cindy anything. And, since I was running out on her, I wasn't going to have much chance to pay her off anyway.

And here I was.

And there was Rhonda.

"Where could we go?"

"I have a place."

"Well…fine. I mean — "

"One thing, Nat. Maybe you'll object, but it is going to cost you. I'm good and I'm selective and I'm worth the money, but it's strictly pay-for-play with me."

It was a surprise but I guess it shouldn't have been. When a girl comes on like that out of the blue she has to be a whore. Not in the books I read, of course, but in life. This is a good world and all, but it's not *that* good.

"How much?"

"Twenty dollars."

It took all of three seconds for the beauty of that to hit me. I suddenly knew what I was going to do with one of the fake twenties I was carrying around. I was going to roll around in the sack with Rhonda King. The notion pleased me immensely.

There is a great deal to be said for paying a whore in counterfeit money. Poetry, kind of. Poetry and rhythm and melody. I was very pleased with myself.

"Twenty," I said, "is fine."

A sucker play? I didn't know. She could take my twenty ahead of time and ditch me. It was a line I would never have fallen for if the twenty involved was real. Since it wasn't, and since I was just going to throw it the hell away anyhow, I didn't much care if I was the mark in a one-woman con game. I'd go along for the ride. I would win even if I lost.

So what the hell.

I found my wallet, slipped out a twenty, folded it and passed it to her under the table. She opened it, looked down at it, and smiled. She was a happy girl. I wasn't going to take the fun out of it for her.

"Let's go, Nat."

"I don't have a car."

"I do. Come on."

I came on, out of the bar to the street, down the street to her car. It was a pretty fancy car for a whore but then she was a pretty fancy whore. The car was a big black Mercury. She drove and I sat next to her.

I kept my hands busy. She either liked it or put up a good act, and I decided that I was getting my money's worth even if we didn't wind up in bed. I slipped one arm around her and filled up one hand with breast — firm solid flesh, fine flesh. She must have been a prewar model, I remember thinking, because they didn't try to save material when they put her together.

I put the other hand up her skirt and found out that she didn't believe in underwear. It was a happy discovery. Happy for both of us, I suppose, because she was having a little trouble with the car. She kept squirming in her seat and tightening her thighs around my hand and a couple of times she damn near lost control of the car.

"Nat," she breathed. "Oh, we are going to have fun. We are going to have lots of fun."

120

She didn't know the half of it.

At a streetlight she turned and came into my arms for a long kiss. It was a jolly one, believe me. The Phoenix citizenry must have had fun watching us ignore the fact that it was broad daylight out. And we ignored the bejesus out of it.

I did something with one of my hot hands and she let out a little moan. It sounded nice and I did it again and she moaned again.

"You better hurry," I managed to say. "Or we won't get to your place. We'll have our jollies here."

"Here?"

"In the car," I said. "In the middle of the street."

"Sounds like fun."

"Probably illegal, though."

"But lots of fun—"

I made myself let go of her and told her to drive. She drove, then parked, then got out of the car and told me to come with her. I didn't need a second invitation.

On the way up the stairs I thought that I shouldn't be that excited. Hell, she was only a whore. And whores just aren't all that exciting. Cash on the line is no basis for love.

The hell of it was this—it didn't seem like a cash deal. It took me half the walk upstairs to figure out why. The reason was simple—this wasn't a cash thing, it was seduction. One of those seductions where the victim is getting faked out. And Rhonda, or whatever in hell her name might have been, was definitely getting faked out.

We reached the top of the staircase and I reached for her. She turned to me and all of her was next to all of me. My chest was very warm where her breasts were pressed tight against me. My hands were also warm—they cupped her buttocks and held her close. And my mouth was on fire—her tongue was in it and her tongue knew ingenious tricks.

"This it?"

I pointed at a door. She nodded. This, it seemed, was indeed it. And it was a damn good thing. I could not have climbed another flight of stairs. But I wondered why she was just sort of standing there, not getting ready to open the door. Hell, I wanted to get the show on the road.

"Nat—"

"C'mon," I said, running my hands over her body. I touched interesting parts of her and grinned ghoulishly. "C'mon, dammit. I can't wait much longer."

"Okay," she said. "You first."

And she pointed at the door. I walked to it, wrapped my hand around the door's knob, which couldn't compare with hers, and thought about opening the door. Strange that it wasn't locked. But then a whore wouldn't keep her door locked. Not unless she was afraid of somebody stealing her basin. Of course, there was always the chance that I would step inside and get hit on the head. But I was willing to take the chance. I opened the door and stepped inside.

I didn't get hit on the head.

That would have been too easy.

Instead I stared at three men and two guns. I didn't recognize one man or either gun, but the other two men were fellows I had seen before.

Reed.

And Baron.

"Inside," Reed was saying. "And shut the door, Lindsay. We don't want to be disturbed."

8

"Good going, Lori. You, Lindsay — don't move. Just stand there. And start talking."

A bell rang somewhere in the back of my head. Lori? The bell murmured something about a girl named Lori Leigh. Cindy had described her as blonde and busty, which was certainly a pretty accurate description of my girl Rhonda. I'd given up Lori Leigh as a bad dream about the time when Cindy's story started coming up roses. I had made a mistake.

"I found him in a bar," Lori was saying now. "Told him I made it for money. He gave me a twenty."

"A live one?"

"One of ours."

The men laughed. "Too much." Baron said. He was even bigger than I remembered, a mountain of a man with a head like a boulder. "Paying you off in queer. That moves me."

Reed I've mentioned before — medium height, medium build, sandy hair. He looked as though he was the type who poured boiling oil on troubled waters. The guy who rounded out the party looked like the oil itself. A little greaseball with eyes that stared dead ahead.

Baron came up to me. He was smiling and I decided maybe they weren't such bad guys after all. He held out a hand and I reached to take it.

I missed. And he hit me in the chest.

"Funny man," he said. "You better talk, funny man. There's a little bit of fifty grand you got and that we want. There's a little frail named Cindy who has to be taken apart at the seams. You got talking to do."

I felt around and found out my ribs were still there. It should have been reassuring. It wasn't.

"Lindsay?" Reed's voice. I looked up. "You got two choices; Lindsay. You can let us work on you until you spill or you can spill now and save us the trouble. That way you came out of it with your teeth in your head. Either way you want it, Lindsay. Just tell us."

Choices, yet. I opened my mouth to tell him what he could go and do to himself, then thought it over for a minute and let my mouth drop shut. I was in a bind, trapped like a rat in a rat trap. And for what? A girl who conned me? Money I wasn't planning on spending anyway?

Two dumb things to get killed for.

I stood up. Baron moved in, ready to pound my face in. He threw the punch before I could start talking and my head took off and waltzed around the room. I almost went out, but not quite. I went to the floor and stayed there while my head came back to me again.

"What do you say, Lindsay?"

"I'll talk." I said. "Hell, the broad conned me to begin with. I was ready to powder and leave her with the dough. I got no reason to hold out."

Reed didn't say anything.

I pointed at Baron. "You can tell this bastard a couple things. You can tell him he didn't have to hit me. Not the first time and not the second time. You can also tell him that one of these days I'm going to kill him."

Baron laughed.

"Look," Reed said, "we want a couple things. We want the girl and we want the money. And some information."

"I can take you to her. Or do you want the information first?"

He thought it over. "That makes more sense. Start talking."

"Where do I start?"

"With the money," Reed said. "How much of it is left?"

"There was fifty grand to start with?"

He nodded.

"Maybe a thousand of that is gone. Part of that in New York, the rest here in Phoenix. The rest is still in the little black bag the way it was when I ran into her."

"Good. How did you meet her?"

I hesitated, then told him. I left out most of it, just giving him the picture of a good-natured slob who got tied up with a frantic frail without knowing entirely what was going on. I saw a few reasons for feeding him the story. For one thing, it happened to be pretty much the truth. For another, the less involved I was, the less chance there would be of them deciding to kill me. And, of course, Cindy had suckered them. This would put us both in the same boat. The boat would be rocky as New England soil, but it just might float.

"You thought the dough was straight?"

"That's right."

"How did you tumble?"

I told him that, too. I ran through it, told him how she was acting funny so I ran a check on her story and came out with more questions than answers. He got very interested when I went through the routine at the bank, how I checked the bill and managed to get away with it. I think he seemed impressed.

"For a mark," he said. "you came out of it okay. You got a head, anyway."

"And fists," Baron said. "You did a job on Bunkie. That wasn't nice."

I told Baron where he should stick himself. He came on to me and I got ready to take another punch. But Reed motioned the big man away.

"Let's get back to Cindy," he said. "She's got the dough?"

"She and the dough are in the room."

"So let's go."

So we went. Down the stairs and out to the street and into the same damned car that Rhonda—I mean Lori—had used for fun and games. That, I decided, was one thing I would always regret. I hadn't managed to knock off a piece of Lori. It was one hell of a shame.

In the car I had questions. "How did you find us?" I asked. "I don't remember leaving a trail."

"Cindy tipped us. A wire day before yesterday."

It figured. "Another question," I said. "You're going to a hell of a lot of trouble for fifty grand in schlock. You're spending that much more to get it back. Maybe I'm stupid, but I don't get it. Wouldn't it make more sense to spend the time printing up fresh stuff?"

Reed and Baron looked at each other. I looked at the two of them, then at the greaseball who was doing the driving, then at Lori. Lori was the only one who was any fun to look at.

"Might as well tell him," Reed said. "Can't hurt."

He turned to me. "We were working together," he said. "Cindy was part of the racket. You know about the paper, don't you? The process?"

"I know what you do. Not how, but what. You bleach singles and print twenties on them."

"That's about it. We had the process, had a set of plates. The plates were good."

"Very good."

"But not perfect," Reed said. "There were a couple errors there, nothing big, but big enough to make the bills obviously counterfeit to an expert with an eye in his head. We weren't going to run those plates. I had a boy coming who was a hell of a touch with engraver's tools. Give him a few days with the plates and no one in the world could tell the queer from the straight. You seen our bills?"

I nodded. Seen them? Hell, I'd been *spending* them.

"Then you know how good they are. The paper is good and the plates are close to perfect. We even have automatic switchers for the serial numbers so they can't pull the bills by number. But the plates weren't perfect and we were waiting until the boy could fix that for us."

I was beginning to bet a glimmer.

"Cindy," Reed said bitterly. "Big ideas and small brains. Her cut wasn't enough for her. She had to put the plates on the rotary one night when everybody else was decked out. She was smooth, that girl. Stupid but smooth. She inked and rolled and churned out a quick fifty grand. And lammed before anybody woke up."

I was beginning to see things. But it still didn't add up, not all across the board. "Look," I said, "it's still only fifty grand. Once your boy makes the scene you can print up better stuff, as much of it as you want. So why chase her down for the fifty? Point of honor or something?"

Reed shook his head, impatient. "Same plates," he said. "If the schlock she's carrying turns up phony, some joker can compare it with our stuff and put two and two together. And come up with four."

"Oh," I said.

"See? She's got fifty grand in counterfeit dough. She wants double that for it. It's a real live one, Lindsay. For the first time ever counterfeit is worth twice as much as straight money. One for the books, huh?"

Now it made sense.

"This isn't a minor-key operation, Lindsay. This isn't a hit-and-run game, with one roll off the plates and no more. This is enough to keep a bunch of people for life. Cindy has us strangled."

"So you have to get the money back."

"Right," he said. "She isn't working a deal. She's blackmailing us. She's got us over a barrel but she's over a barrel herself. Three times now she's tried to make the connection with us. We get on the scene and she changes her mind, runs like a rabbit. We can't roll our own stuff until we get hers back."

"There's already a thousand in circulation."

"Peanuts," Baron said. "It's good schlock. Half of it won't ever turn up. And without her holding it, nobody can connect it with us. So we're clear."

I had a pretty good idea what they were going to do to Cindy. She wasn't going to stay alive, not for long. I was starting to feel sorry for her. Hell, she'd pulled some pretty switches on me. But I could see her point. She was desperate and I was handy. What else could she do?

That wasn't all. She'd been good to me. She could have powdered, could have been less fun in bed — there were plenty of ways I could have wound up on the short end of the stick. She wasn't being honest with me but that was her privilege. I didn't want Baron working her over, killing her.

They were going to kill her, that was certain. And, I realized, they were probably going to do as much for me. That's why it wouldn't hurt to tell me all this.

My knees felt very weak.

"This the hotel?"

I nodded. The greaseball pulled the big car over to the curb and we got out of it. I walked first, with Reed right behind me. I wondered what chances I had of making a break for it. There was no gun showing but I knew there was one held on me. And they wouldn't mind shooting.

"Don't try it," Reed said, reading my mind. "Walk straight into the lobby and into the elevator. Then go right into her room. Or you're dead."

I'm stupid, but only up to a certain point. I didn't want a bullet in the back, not just then. I walked into the lobby and over to the elevator, trying to look suspicious. For once I wanted all the cops in the world to notice me. If the cops came, Reed wouldn't shoot. He would be caught, and I would be caught, and being caught was greatly to be preferred to being dead.

But, of course, no cops came.

The elevator took us to our floor. We walked to the room and I stood in front of the door waiting for something nice to happen to me. Nothing nice happened.

"Knock," Reed suggested.

I knocked, hoping that she wouldn't answer the door. Maybe she would sleep nice and soundly, and not answer the door, and we could go away and let her live.

She didn't answer the door. I turned to Reed, shrugged mightily, and he wasn't amused. "You got a key," he snapped. "Use it."

I had a key and used it. I half hoped the key wouldn't work, but the key did work, and I opened the door, and Cinderella Sims was nowhere to be seen.

"Not here," Baron said. It was, for Baron, a pretty brilliant observation.

"Probably out shopping," I suggested. "She goes shopping a lot."

"Spending our money?

"Generally."

"We'll wait," Reed said. He made himself comfortable on top of the bed. I remember thinking that he was not the first person to be comfortable on that particular bed. Two others had been so—Ted Lindsay and Cinderella Sims. That made me very sad, thinking about what was going to happen to Cindy. And, for that matter, to me. There had to be something I could do, but whatever it was, I wasn't aware of it.

Then I thought of something else. Reed was sitting approximately eighteen inches above the fifty grand he was so hot to get his pretty little hands on. That gave me something to think about. All he had to do was look under the bed and he didn't need me around any more. Reed or Baron would put me out of the way. Then they could wait for Cindy and kill her. We lost either way, but the longer I kept him from finding the money, the longer I stayed alive. And who was to say what could happen in the meanwhile? Maybe the police would break the door down. Maybe the Marines would land. Maybe Reed and Baron and Lori and Greaseball would tumble over with heart attacks. Maybe—

"Lindsay?"

I looked at him.

"The money," he said. "The schlock: The little black bag. Get it now. Then we can all wait for the girl."

"I don't know where she put it."

"Get it Lindsay."

"I'm telling you, I don't—"

Baron hit me and the rest of my sentence was forever lost. I came up mad and went at him. He clubbed me again and this time I stayed on the floor for quite awhile.

"The money, Lindsay."

I got up shakily, then pointed under the bed. "That's where she keeps it. You want it so bad you can get it yourselves."

Which is what they decided to do. Baron and Greaseball each took an end of the bed while Reed stood up and kept a gun trained on me. They picked up the bed, carried it out of the way, set it down again. I didn't even watch. I was waiting for them to go into orbit when they saw the money.

They went into orbit, all right. They went into orbit when they *didn't* see the money.

So did I.

My little Sunflower had taken it on the lam. Dough and all, sweet little Cindy Sims had run out on me. I didn't feel too good all of a sudden.

"I'll beat it out of him," Baron was saying. "He'll talk. He'll talk through broken teeth, but he'll talk."

Baron wasn't kidding. But he was wrong. He would beat me, and I would not talk at all. I wouldn't have a thing in the world to talk about.

Which wouldn't bother Baron. He'd just keep knocking the crap out of me, and he would keep on going until I was dead, then they'd go out hunting for Cindy, chasing the golden fleece of the fifty grand in queer that could put them away for the rest of their lives.

I watched Baron come in and got ready for another punch. Then something snapped inside me. I wasn't going to take another beating no matter what happened. A bullet couldn't hurt a hell of a lot worse than one of Baron's punches. At least I would die trying. Either way I would be dead, but this would be faster and easier and a lot more exciting.

"Don't hit me, Baron."

"You ready to talk?"

"There's nothing to say."

He had a gun in one hand, Reed's gun, and this time he decided to give me the gun in the teeth. I suppose he figured I would stand there and wait for it.

He figured wrong.

He swung and I ducked and came up under the arm, fastening my hand on it and pivoting. Baron went across the room and into the wall, landing head first. The gun remained with me, which was the general object of the whole thing.

Lori was close to me, which was her mistake. I grabbed her just in time, held her in front of me and kept my gun pointed at Greaseball. He had the only other gun in the room and he couldn't shoot without hitting Lori. I held onto her and her fright was a live thing in the room. She was scared stiff, shaking and quaking.

I found out why.

Greaseball wasn't the sentimental type. Lori was between me and his gun, so he did the obvious thing under that set of circumstances.

He shot her.

She let out a very sick moan, and then I was holding a heap of dead flesh instead of a live and lovely woman. It was something sick to think about but I didn't waste time thinking. There were more important things to do.

I shot Greaseball in the throat and watched him die.

"Don't do it, Reed."

He was halfway to Greaseball's gun when my voice stopped him. He hesitated for a minute, then straightened up. I had him cold.

"Don't move," I said. "Stay right there. It's nice and cozy there. You can relax and enjoy yourselves."

I kept my gun on them while I backed out the door, then slammed it fast and turned the key in the lock. I left the key there and hoped it would give them a hard time. With luck the police would get there just at the right time—before Reed and Baron got out and after I was far away.

With luck.

I passed up the elevator and took the stairs two and three at a time. I never moved so fast in my life. I was at the second floor when I heard the noise.

A gunshot. Reed, probably, shooting the lock off the door. I should have taken his gun.

The hell with it. You can't think of everything.

I got out of the lobby and into the street. God knows how. If anybody looked suspicious, I did. And if anybody was all dressed up with no place to go, I was. No car, no money, no nothing. I should have stayed up there and let Baron beat me to death.

Their car.

That would do it—give me an out and take their car away from them all at once. Maybe they had left the keys in it. It always happens that way in the movies. But, dammit, I wasn't in a movie. Still, you never could tell. I looked around and found their car and ran at the big Mercury at top speed, trying at the same time to look nonchalant as all hell. I don't think I managed it.

The car was there. And the keys, God bless 'em, were still resting gently in the ignition.

That wasn't all. There was another extra dividend in the car.

A woman.

"Get in, Ted. Don't waste any time. There's no time, hurry, you've got to hurry. I'll explain later. Just get in the car."

Cindy.

She drove even better than she made love. We got out of downtown Phoenix, out of residential Phoenix, out of suburban Phoenix, out of Phoenix entirely. She kept the gas pedal as close to the floor as she could and I looked out of the rear window for cops and robbers. It seemed inevitable that one or the other would catch up with us. We led a charmed life. We left Phoenix behind and I almost relaxed.

"Okay," I said. "Now you talk."

She sighed. "I suppose I have to. How much do you know already?"

"Most of it. I knew most of it before they picked me up. They filled me in on the rest."

I told her what I knew and she nodded. There wasn't anything more. I had all the details.

"You," I said. "You were ditching me, huh? That makes sense, I guess. But why did you stick around and save my neck? That part doesn't make any sense at all."

She took a breath. "I wasn't ditching you."

"Sure. You were waiting for me to join you in the wilds of Transylvania."

"Ted—"

"I'm a big boy now," I said. "You can give it to me straight now, Cindy. You don't have to play games with me anymore. The truth is plenty."

"I'm telling you the truth."

"Sure you are. You never told a lie in your life. Starting with the time you chopped down the cherry tree you've been a model of honesty. Sure."

"Ted—"

"The truth is enough, Cindy. If you'd just—"

"*Damn you!*"

I looked at her. The *damn you!* line had almost sent the car off the road. She was steady now but her eyes were blazing and I could tell how mad she was.

"Listen to me," she said. "Don't interrupt and don't play the little boy that's been getting crapped on from all sides. Just shut up and listen to me."

I shut up and listened to her.

"I wasn't running out," she said. "I knew what was happening the minute I saw you drive by with Lori. You and that perfumed panther."

"*De mortuis,*" I said. "Speak well of the dead."

"She's dead?"

"Dead as silent movies."

"You killed her?"

"Greaseball killed her. Then I shot Greaseball."

"Greaseball? That must be Musso." She described him and the description fit.

"I'm almost sorry Lori's dead," she said, not sounding the least bit sorry. "But you didn't have to hop in with her. You didn't have to be so hot to get next to her."

"That wasn't it," I lied. "She had a gun on me."

"Crap." The word was an explosion. "I saw what you were doing to her in the car. I saw your hands on her."

I looked ashamed.

"So there you were," she said. "You and Lori. And I knew that any minute the whole batch of you were going to pour through the door. What in hell was I supposed to do, Ted? Wait for you? Wait for Baron to beat me to death? Is that what you wanted me to do?"

Strangely enough, I had nothing to say. This sort of changed things. She hadn't been taking a powder on me. I had been two-timing her, and she had every right in the world to be sore.

"I took the bag and left," she said. "I sat in the diner across the street and waited for them to come back. They went upstairs and I got in the car. God knows I shouldn't have waited for you. I should have left then and there and to hell with you. But I waited."

"And saved my life."

"And saved your life. You saved mine once and now we're even. You can leave now if you want. It's been fun, Ted. I like being around you. Maybe I'll drop you a postcard once in a while."

"If you're still alive."

She stared at me.

"Where do you go from here?" I wanted to know. "Going to play the same game? Hide and tip them and run when they catch up with you?"

"Probably."

"You'll run forever," I said. "Or they'll catch you and kill you. Doesn't sound so brilliant to me. Maybe I'm just a dull-witted type, but there has to be an easier way to make a living."

"You got a better way?"

"Maybe."

"Maybe I should throw the money away," she said. "Maybe I should toss it out of the car and to hell with it. A hundred grand. You want me to throw it away, Ted?"

A few hours back I would have answered yes to that. But that was before a lot of things, before Lori died in my arms and before I put a bullet in Musso's throat. Before Baron hit me and before I decided that someday, somehow, I was going to kill him.

"No," I said. "I don't want you to throw it away."

"Then what?"

I thought about it. I had an idea, a good idea.

Maybe.

"Later," I said to her. "Later, when we have more time to talk."

"We? You're still coming along for the ride?"

"I'm still coming," I said. "Later."

"Tell me more, Ted."

I shook my head. "Two questions first. How many more in the mob?"

"Bunkie Craig, the one you put in the hospital. And Casper."

"Who's Casper?"

"A snake," she said. "A weak little man with cold eyes. I never liked him."

There wasn't anybody in the mob worth liking. "Where's Casper?"

"At the hangout."

"And where's that?"

"San Francisco. Why, Ted?"

"Later," I told her. "When there's time for it. You know how to get there?"

"Of course. Why?"

"Later," I said again. "First there's something else we have to get out of the way. See that motel?"

She nodded.

"Pull over," I said. "Lock the schlock in the trunk. And come with me. We're going to make love."

She pulled over and locked the schlock in the trunk and followed me into the office.

It was life again, living again, seeing and hearing and tasting and smelling and touching again.

It was the world.

It had been good with her before. But now it was like nothing before, like nothing ever. Now she was hiding nothing, concealing nothing, holding nothing back from me. Now she was mine and I was hers, and we were together now and forever, and it was very good.

We made it take a long time. I undressed her, with the lights out in the motel room and soft light filtering through from the half-open closet door. I took off her clothes slowly and ran my hands over that body, that perfect body, letting my hands linger where they liked to linger.

Then she undressed me.

I kissed her and it was good. Her mouth was warm and sweeter than wine. Her arms were around me and her body was very warm, very sweet, very firm and soft and perfect against my body.

"Ted—"

My hands found her breasts, held them, stroked them. The nipples stood at attention and saluted. I kissed them and she started to squirm.

"Now, Ted!"

But not yet. Not for awhile, not for an eternity, not until neither of us could stand waiting any longer. Not until the world flew by at half-mast.

Then it was time. It began.

There were sounds outside that I did not hear. They didn't matter. There was a world outside but it existed for me no longer. There was a woman beneath me and she was the only important entity in God's world.

She moaned my name, moaned once and twice and three times. I clutched her and held her and loved her with every atom of my being. It was getting better now, getting to a peak where no adjectives applied, getting to perfection. And you cannot describe perfection.

You can only enjoy it.

The peak approached and blinded us. We were there together now, to the very top of the world. Then, all at once, there was no world beneath us.

Only Cindy and I, alone together, floating in free fall in space.

It was over. I held her while she cried salty tears.

I lay on my back and thought about things. I thought about the way I had led Reed and Baron to her, lead them to her room so that they could kill her.

And hated myself.

I knew something now. I knew that we were together as long as we lived, knew that nobody on earth could keep us apart. I knew that the world was our world now, that it belonged to us, that we had it by the tail.

"Ted?"

I took her hand.

"What you were going to tell me," she said. "You can tell me now."

She was right. Now we had no secrets.

I took a deep breath, let it out slowly. I reached over for the cigarettes on the night table, lit two of them and gave one to her. For several moments we smoked side by side in silence.

"Okay," I said slowly. "Here it is."

9

We left the car there in the morning. It was hot and we didn't need it any more. That wasn't all we left behind. We left the twenties.

In ashes.

We burned them in the motel room, burned a few bills at a time in the john and flushed the ashes in the toilet. Have you ever watched close to fifty grand converted into smoke and ashes?

It's quite a sight.

We saved a couple bills. Not many. Enough for food and hotel bills and bus fare to San Francisco. That was all we needed. Any more would have been taking chances.

We weren't taking any chances.

We left the car and we left the motel and we left the ashes. We walked down the road to the nearest town. It had a bus stop. The bus made a few stops until it reached a town that had a little more to say.

The bus from that town went to Frisco. We were on it, tense and excited and a little scared. Not too scared. We were growing up, Cindy and I. It was going to take a lot to scare us. Parts of us were steel, tough and strong.

"It's a chance," she said.

"We've taken plenty of them. We've taken worse chances than this one. We've stuck our necks out in front of Reed and Baron. This is nothing next to that."

"I know."

"This is the only way," I told her. "You can look at it mathematically. It's an equation."

"A human equation."

"Maybe. Maybe two and two is four. Maybe something a lot more complex than that. But it adds up just the same. It adds up and makes sense."

"I know, Ted."

"The phony stuff. The fifty grand. It was worth plenty to Reed and Baron. Worth double its face value. But it was strictly a closed market, baby. A closed market is a buyer's market. You didn't have something you could turn around and sell to anybody else. Reed was the only customer. And he wasn't buying. He was going to kill for it."

I lit a cigarette. I wasn't sure whether or not you could smoke on the bus. It was one of those hick bus lines, not Greyhound or anything, and for all I knew smoking wasn't allowed. I didn't really care. "So you played it the only way. Getting in touch with him, getting him to come down, then running when he showed. Didn't make much sense, but then neither did anything else."

"He was the only customer."

"That's just it," I said. "This way it's different. What Reed has is what's valuable. Especially with the bad stuff gone. Now his plates and his paper can set somebody up for life. With no chance involved."

"Somebody like us," she breathed. It was a prayer. I hoped it would be answered.

"Somebody like us. Somebody very much like us, in fact. All we have to do is take it."

"Sure," she said. "That's all."

I put out the cigarette. "We can manage it," I said. "Let's go over it again. Casper's the only one at the hangout?"

"As far as I know. Bunkie Craig may be there. If he's out of the hospital."

"Is that where he would go?"

She nodded.

"He might be out. It'll be just as well that way, come to think of it; get him out of the way. Nobody else knows about the deal?"

"Just the guy who fixed the plates."

"What about him?"

"He won't talk," she said softly. "I read about him a few days ago. They found his body in a ditch. Reed doesn't believe in letting people know too much. Not unless they're with him all the way. The boy was hired, then fired, then dead. That's how it goes with Reed."

"Four left," I said. "Reed and Baron, Casper and Craig. Lori and Musso are dead. Just the four of them."

"Four," she echoed.

"Four. Then you and me and the money. No set sum, Cindy. As much as we ever want. As much as we ever need."

Thinking about the kid Reed had killed must have jarred her a little. It showed in her face. Not obviously, but I knew her well enough to see it.

"We could just get out of it," she said. "We burned the money. They don't have to chase us any more."

"You really think so?"

She looked at me.

"They'll chase us until we're dead." I said. "Because they don't know we burned that money. Because we know more than they want us to know. We can't beg out now. We either go through with it or run like rabbits."

"You're right," she said. "I'm sorry, Ted."

"That's okay."

"I don't think sometimes."

"Forget it."

I held her hand and lit two more cigarettes.

We were tired when we hit Frisco. Tired enough to sleep. Not because we wanted to sleep, not because we wanted to waste any time. Because we had to be rested, had to be fit when we laid it on the line.

And there were plans to make. I bought a box of shells for the gun, practiced with it empty so I would be able to aim it straight. Hitting Musso had been dumb luck. I'd have to be good this time.

Then we hit the sack. We stayed at a second-grade hotel — good enough so we wouldn't draw stares, cheap enough so we could afford it.

And close to the hideout.

The gang's headquarters was a frame house on Grand Street, a clapboard affair that needed painting badly. I got a look at it from the cab. It looked like any other house on the block, no better, no worse — and certainly no more likely to hold a counterfeiting printing press and a gang of thieves. I caught my breath when I looked at it. I wondered who the neighbors were, what Reed did when door-to-door salesmen dropped by. Things like that.

And I could feel the excitement. We were close now, too close to turn back, ready to roll. I had a tough time sitting still. That's how I react to tension. I get a surplus of nervous energy and there has to be a way to dissipate it. I felt like hitting somebody but there was nobody handy to hit. There would be. Later.

I wiggled my toes, snapped my fingers, felt silly doing it but couldn't sit still otherwise. Cindy gave the cabby the hotel's address and we went back there and sacked out.

"Tomorrow," she said. "Right?"

"Right. In the morning. A quick breakfast and we move. We can't waste time."

"Suppose Reed is back already?"

I shook my head. "He won't be," I said. "Not a chance in the world. He'll be looking around for us, putting out feelers. He may have called, though."

"Then Casper will be waiting for us."

I shook my head. "Like hell he will. Nobody will figure us for a move like this. Casper'll be sitting on his behind waiting for something to happen. Alone or with Craig—either way he won't be a problem."

"He knows me."

"He doesn't know me."

"Craig does."

I thought that one over, then shrugged. "That's a chance," I said. "One we can afford to take. I'm gambling that they won't be ready for anything. If they are, it's going to be harder."

That was an understatement. We had one gun, the one I had taken away from Baron. They would have an arsenal. If all four of them were at the place we could throw in the sponge. But that wasn't the way I figured it. Reed and Baron would show the next evening or the morning after, maybe later.

Maybe.

There were too many things to figure. Maybe nobody bothered to write down the method of bleaching ones and turning them into twenties. Maybe there was no ink around, maybe we wouldn't be able to find the plates, a lot of maybes. I didn't want to think about them.

I couldn't afford to think about them.

I put them out of my mind.

There was still Cindy, nervous in spite of herself, nervous if not exactly scared. There was still me, alive with nervous energy, all that energy that had to be dissipated one way or another.

There was still the bed.

It was different that night. It was a frenetic passion, a passion used to chase away fear, passion born of tension and worry and gentle fear. It blazed and it sizzled and it burned like fire.

It was good because it had to be good, because we needed it so desperately, because it was, for the moment, the only thing in the world we could have.

And for another reason.

Because there might be no more chances. Because we might both be dead before we were together in bed again, because the next bed we shared might be a grave or a river bottom or a cold stone slab.

We were naked together, naked in the bed, and when I felt the sweet warm softness of her beside me my mind went blank and my brain started to swim. She made a little moaning sound deep in her throat; then she was in my arms. Her lips opened under mine and I tasted her mouth in a deep, long kiss.

Then our bodies were pressed taut together, straining, and I felt her firm breasts press hard against my chest. She writhed in my arms, and when I kissed her I tasted the salty tang of silent tears.

It all made sense to me now. We'd gone out on a limb, far out on a limb, and now we were going to saw the limb off and leave ourselves hanging in the middle of the air. We weren't going to work deals now, and we weren't going to keep on running, and we weren't going to roll over and play dead like nice little doggies doing nice little tricks. We were taking the bull by the horns and the bit in our teeth, and we stood a damned good chance of winding up holding the tiger by the tail.

"Ted—"

She drew away from me and my hands found her breasts. I looked at her face. Her eyes were shining, glowing with a mixture of love and passion, and her mouth was curled in a sexy smile.

I reached out a finger and touched her lips. She kissed the finger. Then I ran that finger down over her chin and throat, down to her breast. I traced ever-diminishing concentric circles around her breast, with the circles getting smaller and smaller until I was touching her nipple and driving her wild.

The change in her was dramatic. Now she was a creature on fire, basic woman incarnate, a thrashing melody of hips and thighs and rampant breasts.

"Ted—"

144

We were on our way to the gang's hideout, on our way to outfox the foxes. We were kiddies playing cops and robbers, with a big payoff for the winners and a shallow grave for the losers.

But now this didn't matter.

Not now.

Not for the time being.

Because now she was in my arms, soft and warm and willing, and now she was the only thing in the world that mattered. I was kissing her breasts now. She was churning spasmodically and the earth was in the grip of a cyclone that could pick us up and whirl us away to the land of Oz.

My lips bathed the silken skin. Then I moved lower, coaxing her into delicious peals of torment, kissing the smooth sleek satiny flatness of her body. She wound her fingers in my hair and I thought for a moment she was going to snatch me baldheaded.

I wouldn't have noticed if she had.

I was too busy.

We were going to be criminals, but crime and punishment were a million miles away by now. We were going to be thieves in the night, but now we were naked in the night and the night was a handful of stars in the palm of an angry goddess.

"Ted, I love you! Don't stop, Ted. Don't ever stop. Do it forever!"

She didn't have to say a word. I was not going to stop, not now and not ever. I was giving her the ultimate kiss, the kiss that would seal all bargains until the end of time. Nothing else mattered.

Nothing at all.

And then I was giving her that kiss.

Her whole body was twitching and shaking and heaving, and the heat she was generating would have melted the polar ice cap and vaporized the ensuing water. The passion was a contagious sort of thing and the room was the scene of an epidemic in no time at all.

I needed her, had to have her, and now the kiss was not enough, just as nothing could be enough.

It was time.

And then it began.

I've already said it was good, and that's about all I can say. It was the beginning and the end of the world. It was a pair of bodies drawn to one another like magnets, clutching and clinging, working rapidly and relentlessly, making moves and seeing stars and breaking records.

"Ted, I love it. Ted, I love it I love you I love everything!"

I loved everything, too.

And it got better and better and better, and it got faster and faster and faster, until it had to stop or it would almost certainly have killed us both.

Then the explosion came. The earth began to tremble and shake, and guns went off and rockets shot up and satellites went into orbit.

And so did we.

Then, after a fashion there was calmness. Then I was holding her in my arms saying meaningless things to her. And then I knew that we were going to go through with it, going to go through with everything, going to take on Reed and Baron and the rest of the mob and come out smelling like a rose.

Nothing could go wrong for us.

Not now.

Not after that.

We lay together, and we touched each other, and we spoke very few words because no words were needed.

Finally we drifted into a hazy, desperate sleep.

Morning came too quickly. There should have been a slow period of awakening, a gentle touching of bodies drugged by sleep, of lovemaking that was all sweetness and animalism and warmth and love.

That's not how it was. It was morning, and sunlight flooded the room, and we made the transference from sleep to consciousness in the shadow of an instant, woke up and blinked once and left the safety of our bed.

"It's time," I said.

We dressed quickly. I shaved, we showered, we put on our clothes and checked out of the hotel. We had breakfast in a diner around the corner, a greasy spoon something like the place where I had slung hash in New York. Grace's Lunch on Columbus Avenue. How long ago had that been? Days? Weeks? Years? It was hard to tell, impossible to believe. It was way back, buried somewhere, over and done with.

I don't remember what I ate that morning. I don't even remember *that* I ate, but I must have. Eggs, probably. But it's only a guess. Whatever it was, I didn't taste it. I got through with it and Cindy finished whatever in hell she had ordered, and we got out of there.

It was a cool grey sort of morning. The streets were relatively empty, the sky overcast, the temperature more than bearable. A good day for watching a football game, something like that.

I wondered whether it would be a good day for murder.

We walked around a corner, walked a block, turned another corner and kept going. I caught sight of the house, the big frame house where everything was going to happen. The money shop.

"That's it, Ted."

"I know."

The gun was in the waistband of my trousers and the jacket hid it. But I could feel it. The metal was very cold, or felt that way.

"How, Ted?"

We'd been over it a dozen times. I spelled it out for her again anyhow.

"Ring the bell, he comes to the door, I push inside. I take care of him, you come in. That's all."

"If there's two of them?"

"Then he recognizes me. Then I get the drop on them. Better give me a hand if I need it. But I won't need it. It'll be smooth as silk. Bunkie or no Bunkie there's not a thing for you to worry about. It's going to be silk-smooth."

Silence. Now we were in front of the house. Time to go in and no sense standing around outside, being seen. Easy to say. Harder to do. She was holding my hand, holding it tight, and maybe the fear she was feeling doubled my own strength. I don't know.

"Ted—"

"Let's go, honey."

"Ted, no killing—"

Half-statement, half-question. She wanted to know and she didn't want to know. I told her no killing. Hell, that was what she wanted to hear. I could always fight with her later, or just go ahead.

Or whatever.

"And no shooting. The neighbors might hear."

"Sure," I said. "Come on, baby."

There was a side door, which was a break. That was the one we picked. I made her stand out of sight while I leaned on the bell. I gave a hell of a lean. If I had things figured right, Casper was still sacked out after a hard night watching the late late show on television and pouring some beer down his throat. If I could get him out of bed it wouldn't hurt the cause any. An opponent with his eyes still closed is the best kind in the world.

"Ted—"

"He'll be coming. Relax."

Relax? Sure.

I heard footsteps outside, spun around and watched the mailman walk past. No mail for the unofficial bureau of engraving and printing. That was good.

Then footsteps from inside. Footsteps coming toward the door. I yanked the gun out of the waistband of my pants and flicked off the safety catch. A voice, thin as a rail, came through the door.

"Who is it?"

"Telegram." What the hell. That's how they always did it in the movies. I wondered what I'd do if he told me to stick it under the door. Probably tell him he had to sign for it. The movies are a great educational institution.

But he didn't play games. He opened the door, his eyes blurry with sleep, and I put the gun in his face. That made the eyes open up some. They went wide with shock and opaque with pure terror.

"Who—"

Casper. He looked like Casper the friendly ghost. His hair was straggly and magnificently uncombed, his face said that a lot of beer went with the late show. He was a mess. A badly shaken mess.

He was wearing pajamas, a pretty simple-looking print with green predominating, and his body showed through. The bones showed. I wondered how different he would look if he were the one with the gun. Then the scared eyes would be killer's eyes and the mouth would foam like a mad dog.

It was good, thinking that way. It kept me from feeling sorry for him.

I shoved him inside, moved in after him. I tried to decide whether to knock him out now or later. Then I remembered Craig. I had to find out if he was around.

"Be cool," I told Casper. "This isn't for you. It's for Bunkie Craig. He around?"

He shook his head but his eyes said yes.

"You better play it straight," I advised him. "Or I kill you by mistake."

"In the bedroom."

"Upstairs or down?"

"Upstairs."

That was fine with me.

"Look, Mac," he whined. "You get Bunkie, huh? Then you let me alone. I'm a right guy. I won't get in your way."

"You don't know the half of it."

"Huh?"

I spoke to her without looking at him. I told her to come on in and she did. It took him three looks at her before he figured it out, remembered who she was, knew all at once that Craig was not the sole reason for our presence.

He became very frightened.

"Turn around, Casper."

He didn't want to. There's something about putting your back to a loaded gun that is most unpleasant no matter who you are and sheer horror if you are a gutless wonder like Casper. But he made it finally, and I hit him.

With the gun. On the side of the head just over the ear. Not hard enough to crack the skull, not so gentle that he could stay awake. He fell soundlessly, doubled up and pitched forward on his face. I figured he'd be out for half an hour but I was taking no chances.

"Watch him," I told her. "If he moves so much as an eyelash, belt him one."

"With what?"

I looked at her. "Your shoe," I said. "Take it off right now."

She was a good kid and she didn't ask questions. She took off her shoe. It had a spike heel that you could drive a tent-stake with. It was better than a sap.

"Now sit down next to him," I said. "And hold the shoe by the toe. If he moves, hit him in the head. Not too hard but hard enough."

Maybe it was melodrama, kneeling next to an unconscious man and all ready to hit him if he groaned. Melodrama is better than dying. We were taking enough chances to begin with. I left her with Casper and started looking for Craig.

The downstairs was a cyclone's aftermath. Casper was a lousy housekeeper. There were beer cans all over the floor, paper plates on the tables with uneaten food still on them, general disorder throughout. I wondered how different the place must have looked when Cindy and Lori were living there. Then I thought about Lori, who was dead now. And about Cindy, who had been shacked up with Reed. Those were things I didn't want to think about. Not now.

I found the stairs and took them as quickly and silently as I could. One of them was creaky and I cursed it silently, then kept right on going. The gun in my hand didn't feel cold any more. It was warm now, warm and alive and ready. I hoped I wouldn't have to use it.

I tried two doors before I found Bunkie's bedroom. It was sort of nerve-wracking, believe me. I screwed up my courage, opened a door, and the room was empty. But when I found him I had no worries.

He was asleep.

I must have given him a bad time in New York. He was still wearing bandages and he needed a few new teeth. But on him the bandages looked good.

I stood there waiting for something, God knows what. I suppose I was waiting for him to wake up. It would be easier with him awake, easier and harder at the same tune. But I couldn't let him wake up. It wasn't the bright thing to do, and now I had to do the bright thing all alone. Or else Cindy and I could throw in the sponge.

It was the hardest thing I ever did in my life. At first I froze completely and couldn't do it at all. Then I thought about Reed and Baron, and I thought about Musso and Lori, and I thought about what they all would have done to us. That didn't make it a hell of a lot easier but by then I was through thinking and ready to act.

I hit him with the butt of the gun.

Not gently, like Casper, but hard. Not over the ear, like Casper, but on the bridge of the nose.

Not to knock him out, like Casper.

To kill him.

It wasn't too easy. I don't think I could have hit him a second time, not the way I felt just then. But I didn't have to. Once was enough. I felt bone give under the heavy gun butt and when I picked the gun up I found out that the shape of his skull wasn't the same. There was a slight depression over his nose.

You can kill a man that way with your bare hands if you know how. It's a kill chop, and properly executed you break off a piece of the frontal bone and drive it back into the brain, killing instantly.

It's tough with your bare hand. You have to be good. But when you use the butt of a gun there is nothing to it at all. It's a snap.

I took a breath, let it out, then stuck the gun back in the waistband of my trousers and reached for his pulse. It wasn't a hellishly huge surprise not to find any pulse.

Bunkie Craig was dead.

I stood there for a few minutes and stared at him. I should have felt something—hatred for the corpse, pity, self-disgust, anything. Musso had been different—then he had a gun and so did I, and I had to shoot him to stay alive. Bunkie Craig had been a wounded man asleep and I had made sure he would sleep until Judgment Day.

But I felt nothing, nothing at all. I was a machine, a well-oiled properly primed machine with one goal in mind. I had no tears for Bunkie Craig. They were all for myself if we failed. Then I could cry. Not now.

I turned away from death and left the bedroom, found the stairs again and followed them to the bottom. I walked away from Craig and found Cindy and Casper, my girl watching him like a hawk, my prisoner still out. She looked at me and asked me with her eyes.

"Everything's fine," I said. And wondered if it was or not.

I didn't kill Casper. He had things to tell us, things we had to know. I let him sleep for a few minutes, then dumped a glass of water over his face. It did the trick. He came up sputtering and shaking all at once. It made a pretty picture. When a weak man is helpless it makes him look much less like a crook. I couldn't help wondering how a fish like Casper had gotten involved with hard guys like Reed and Baron. I had a hunch that all I had to do to find out was hand him my gun.

"What do you want?"

"Information," I said. "Some questions."

"Go ahead."

"For a starter," I said, "where's the press?"

"Basement."

"Take us to it."

He got up and led the way. The basement stairs were rickety and the railing shook a little. I kept the gun pointed at the top of his spine every step of the way. He didn't try anything.

"This way."

We followed him to a little room off the main floor. It was pretty impressive. It didn't look like any quick turnover operation. It was professional.

There was an automatic-feed rotary on a workbench, a stack of bleached paper, a few bills. The bills were nice new twenties hot off the presses. Just a few of them, just enough so that Reed could be sure the boy had done his job properly on the plates before he removed him from the picture.

The plates were also there. Plus a whole case of inks, all the inks necessary to print the bills. It was an amazing setup. The press would ink automatically, feed automatically, dispense bills automatically. All you had to do was hook it up and plug it in and watch it roll.

It was lovely.

The plates had number gadgets hooked up, set to turn over each time a bill was printed. No problem of the same serial number on every bill. No switching it by hand between each impression. It was perfect. All I could do was stare at it.

Then I remembered something.

"The paper," I said. "You got the formula for bleaching the paper?"

His eyes got crafty.

"The formula," I said. "Give."

"If I don't?"

"Then you die."

He shrugged. He had a card to play now and he was making the most of it. "I die anyway," he said, guessing rather accurately. "You killed Bunkie. You'll kill me. Why should I make it easy for you?"

"Make it easy for yourself."

"Huh?"

"Think," I said. "Think what happens to you if you don't talk. Think about matches up and down the soles of your feet. Think about thumbs popping your eyes out. Think about taking three days to die."

I hardly recognized my voice. Evidently he did a little thinking, because his face turned a few unpleasant colors and when he spoke his voice wasn't much more than a whisper. "You'd find it anyway," he croaked. "The drawer."

I found the drawer he was talking about and opened it. A slip of paper, a batch of fairly complex directions, a few bottles of chemicals. That had to be it. But I had to be sure it would work.

"Cindy," I said. "You hold the gun. I want to tie him up while I check this out."

I used his belt on him, then let her hold the gun while I carried out the directions. When the brew was ready I took one of the nice fresh twenties and did what I was supposed to do with it. It didn't take long. The bill came out white and pure, not a trace of ink on it.

"It works," I said reverently. Cindy nodded.

I turned to Casper. "More information," I said. "Reed and Baron. You hear from them?"

He hesitated and I glared at him. "A call," he said finally. "Last night."

"What did they say?"

"Not much."

He shrugged again. "They said expect them tonight. Around ten, maybe later."

"Nothing about me or Cindy?"

"Nothing. Just that they hadn't gotten the schlock but that they were going to roll anyway. Reed said he was through chasing wild geese. Something like that."

That was fine. Cindy and I exchanged glances, pleased with the news. The sooner Reed was coming back, the better for us. We didn't want to hang around any longer than we had to. Enough is enough. And Reed and Baron wouldn't be ready for us. They would be fish in a barrel, which was fine with me. It had been hard enough. Plenty hard. Anything that made it easier was fine with both of us.

"I got a favor to ask."

I looked at him.

"Look," Casper went on, "you can do me a big favor. Fair enough?"

"Go ahead."

"Kill me," he said. "Now. I don't want to die but I don't want to wait either. You're not going to let me live. You as much as said so. Get it over with right away, will you? Waiting makes my skin crawl."

There was nothing more he could tell us, nothing I didn't know. He was scum but he deserved that much.

"You sure you want it?"

"I'm sure."

Cindy's hand was on my arm. Killing in a fight was one thing, she was saying silently. Killing Reed and Baron was one thing. But killing a trussed-up man was another thing. She didn't like it a bit. Well, hell, neither did I. But if there was another way open I couldn't see it. If he lived we were done. There were only three of them now, three who knew the score. Reed and Baron and Casper.

They all had to go.

"How do you want it?"

"A bullet."

I shook my head, hating myself. "I don't want to risk the noise."

"Muffle it with a pillow."

I thought about that. Then I remembered Musso, and the slug in him. Same gun. Ballistics. A connection between the two killings.

I shook my head.

"Then hit me," he said. "Knock me out. Then any way you want. Just quick and easy, that's all."

"Ted—"

Cindy didn't like it, didn't like it at all. But I couldn't help it. Casper had had enough already. At least I could make it quick for him.

"Close your eyes."

He closed them. I took the gun from Cindy, reversed it, gave him the butt across the front of the skull. It didn't kill him but it knocked him cold. He slumped in the chair.

"Don't kill him," she said. "Not murder. Please, Ted. We can get away anyway. He's small. He won't chase us."

It was a very simple equation and I spelled it out for her. "If I kill him we have a chance," I said. "If I let him live we die. Any connection is enough to do it. Anything tying us to the rest of them, any witness left alive—that's all we need. Then we're dead. Murder one. The gas chamber in California. You want the gas chamber?"

She didn't.

Neither did I.

I swung the gun again and smashed Casper's head for him.

10

Twelve hours to wait for Reed and Baron. Twelve hours to sit on our hands.

We didn't sit on our hands. We were lucky — there was plenty to do. Packing, for example. We had plenty to take along with us. The press, the plates, the ink, the blank paper, the chemicals.

Before we packed I put the few counterfeit twenties I was still carrying through the chemical bath. I was suddenly sorry I hadn't brought the whole satchel along — the bills were worth a dollar a piece now. They would have made fine blanks. But it wouldn't have been worth the risk of getting picked up with the satchel in our possession.

I also tumbled on a stack of singles — money they hadn't gotten around to bleaching yet. I packed those. I put the twenties already printed up in my wallet. There was a little over three hundred dollars there, enough to take us wherever we were going.

The press had a carrying case of its own and the rest of the stuff fit into an old suitcase someone had thoughtfully left behind. We got everything ready to go. Once Reed and Baron came back anything could happen. There could be gunshots, in which case we would have to leave in a hurry. I didn't want to have to waste any time, not when time was important.

Cindy was calmer now. The human being is a remarkably adjustable mechanism — it can adjust to murder. She still didn't like it, but then neither did I. She accepted it, though. If nothing else, there was consolation in the argument that we hadn't killed anybody remotely worthwhile. Craig and Casper were lice, thieves, murderers.

We too were thieves and murderers. But that was something we didn't want to dwell on.

"We've got to do a job on this house," I told Cindy. "Sooner or later somebody's going to come around and find the stiffs. No one's going to be able to figure out who killed them or why. That's fine. But we can't let the world dope out the fact that there was a counterfeiting operation here. We have to cover up all the traces."

"How do we do it?"

"Room to room," I said. "Attic to basement. If they left any papers around, get rid of them. If they have anything, anything at all that smells of counterfeiting, dump it. Don't pass up a thing."

She nodded, then suddenly looked very worried. I asked her what was the matter.

"Fingerprints," she whispered. "All over the place. We'll have to wipe them off."

I got a mental picture of the two of us trying to wipe our prints off of everything we may or may not have touched. "Hold on," I said. "Get a grip on yourself. Have you ever been arrested for anything?"

She shook her head.

"Ever hold a government job? Ever get fingerprinted for any reason at all?"

"No."

"Ever in the WACs? WAVEs? Anything like that?"

"Of course not."

"Then relax," I told her. "If your prints aren't on file there's no worry there. If they pick us up they can tie us in, but if they pick us up we're dead anyway. We wouldn't keep our mouths shut very long."

"But—"

"Listen to me," I said. "No one in the world knows about us. No one can tie us in. We hit and we run and we're clear. All the fingerprints in the world won't do them any good. They'll never catch us and they'll never print us. Forget fingerprints. Just make sure there are no traces behind us. I don't want anybody looking for counterfeit twenties."

We started in the attic and we worked our way to the basement. There wasn't a hell of a lot to clean up but we didn't miss any bets. Reed was one of those planners, a compulsive note-taker. Most of his stuff was meaningless to anybody but Reed. I burned it anyway.

There were a few impressions of the original plates lying around, bad stuff that would pass but wasn't perfect. It went in the chemical bath, then in the suitcase. Every room and every closet got careful attention. It did two things—it covered our tracks, most important, and it also gave us something to do. That was important in itself. You can go batty in an empty house waiting for something to happen. This way we kept moving, kept working.

"Ted—"

"What?"

"We've got to do something about the bodies."

She was right. If they were out of the way, there was the chance that somebody could get suspicious, enter the house, and leave without tumbling to the fact that it held four corpses. I didn't have any tremendous desire to lug dead bodies around but it was necessary. I had to get them out of the way, put them someplace dark and quiet.

Bunkie Craig was heavy. I lugged him up to the attic, found an empty trunk and stuck him in it. I closed the trunk and locked it.

And hoped the smell wouldn't seep through when he started to rot.

Casper was light, easy. He was in the cellar already and I didn't particularly want to drag him up all those flights of stairs. He fit in the furnace, snug and cozy. Thank God it was summer. I hoped they would find him before they lit the furnace.

And then there was nothing to do. I broke the gun, checked it, closed it up again. We had too many hours to go and we were nervous. Not frightened, not scared, just tense. Very tense. I wished Reed and Baron would hurry up.

"Ted—"

I looked at her.

"We have the stuff," she said. "We could leave now. We could just get out and run."

"And forget about Reed and Baron?"

"Why not, Ted? We could forget them. They'd never find us. They'd be stuck here and we wouldn't have to take any chances."

I looked at her. "We could run," I said.

"That's right."

"And run and run and run. For the rest of our lives. Is that what you want, Cindy?"

She didn't say anything.

"Running forever. Running and never feeling safe. Always having Reed and Baron somewhere in the background. Always worrying over it, always wondering when they were going to turn up and kill us. That what you want?"

"Ted—"

"Not that way," I said. "Besides, we couldn't ever run. How far do you think we'd get without a car?"

"A car?"

"We're taking their car," I said. "Reed has a new car by now. Not a stolen one. He wouldn't take chances like that. It's an odds-on bet he already bought a car, a properly inconspicuous car. If we're taking the plates and the press and everything, we need a car."

"I suppose so."

"And we have to kill them," I went on. "We have to kill them or die trying. I'd rather die now, here, than wait for them to find us and kill us."

"You're right," she said.

"Of course I am."

"I guess I wasn't thinking."

"You're nervous," I said. She wasn't the only one. There were two of us.

We killed the lights at six o'clock and sat waiting for them. It was dramatic as all hell. I crouched by the window with the shade up about an inch and kept my eye at the opening waiting for something to happen. Every once in a while she would spell me at the window.

Time crawled along and so did my skin. By seven we weren't talking any more. We weren't mad at each other or anything like that. It was just that talking only made everything that much harder to take: Silence was better, silence and our own private thoughts.

A few minutes past eight the phone rang. It rang seven times while we sat and panicked. Then it stopped, and a minute later it rang again.

And stopped after five rings.

I prayed Reed wouldn't be suspicious. Maybe he would figure they were out for a bite, or sleeping, or drunk. Then again maybe he could figure it was us. It was far-fetched but the guy was by no means stupid.

So I prayed.

Nine o'clock.

Nine-thirty.

Ten.

Ten-thirty.

A quarter-to-eleven a car pulled into the driveway. At first I thought it was somebody else turning around but the car went straight into the garage. It was an Olds, two or three years old, black.

Lawrence Block

Two men inside. I saw their faces as they went by.
Reed and Baron.

I lowered the shade the rest of the way and Cindy and I
headed for the side door. Then I remembered there was a back
door and ran to the window. That's where they were heading.
We went to meet them.

I took out the gun, held it so tightly I was afraid the metal
would melt in my hand. We stood behind the door and waited.
I could hear Cindy breathing and I wanted to tell her to stop. It
was that type of scene.

Then I heard them talking.

"Punks. Probably stoned out of their heads, too blind to
answer the phone. You tie up with punks and you got to expect that."

That was Baron. Then Reed: "I don't know. I don't like it.
Craig's a lush half the time but I expect better from Casper."

"A punk."

"I still don't like it. There's something in the air. I can damn
near smell it."

I didn't like it either. Why didn't the son of a bitch open the
door already?

Baron's voice: "C'mon, we don't have all night. Open the
damn door already."

A key scratched its way into the keyhole, turned the lock.
The door opened halfway and I stood behind it, unable to
breathe. They came in slowly, moved past me. I wanted to shoot
but I didn't dare. Not with the door open.

I swung the gun.

It caught Reed on top of the head and sent him to the floor.
Baron turned and I had the gun on him. "Don't move," I said.
"Or you're dead."

"Lindsay!"

"Don't move," I croaked. "Stand where you are."

162

He looked at the gun and ignored it. He came at me like a bull and gave me a shove. Somehow I held onto the gun — but I went halfway across the room.

I pointed the gun at him, aimed it at his chest. The son of a bitch didn't give a damn. He charged right at me, head down, arms out.

I wanted to shoot and I couldn't. It was all over now, I thought. All over but the dying.

He was almost on me. I sidestepped just in time, brought the gun down as hard as I could on top of that thick skull of his. I got lucky. I connected.

It didn't knock him out. That would have been too much to hope for. But it stunned him and that, as it turned out, was enough.

He was on hands and knees, steadying himself for another move. I looked at him and I hated him. Craig and Casper had been necessary but this was a pleasure. I hated Baron, hated him for the beatings and the threats, hated him for the miserable bastard he was. I didn't even have time to reverse the gun in my hand. I had to hit him with the muzzle, and I hit him and hit him and hit him. His skull was like rock but the gun barrel was harder. I beat him across the top of his fat head until he was dead.

Reed.

I had forgotten him and I looked up expecting to get shot any minute. I saw Reed then. There was a gun in his hand.

There was also a knife in his back.

"He was going to shoot you, Ted. I couldn't give him a chance. I — "

She was in my arms, soft and warm and crying. I held her and stroked her and told her everything was going to be all right now. She calmed down, finally.

"I love you," I told her.

She forced a smile. "I'm all right now," she said. "It's just that I never killed a man before. That's all."

First I washed the knife and put it in a drawer in the kitchen. Then I found a closet for Reed and stuck him in it. There was very little blood on the floor—she had gotten lucky and stuck the thing in the spine, killing him at once. I mopped up what blood there was and put the bloody rag in the closet with Reed.

Baron weighed a ton and I felt like leaving him there. It was a good thing the house was lousy with closets. Cindy gave me a hand with him and we put him away for awhile.

Then we got the hell out of there. I carried the press and the suitcase, left the gun in the closet with Baron, loaded the stuff in the trunk of the car. The keys weren't in the ignition and I had to go back and get them from Reed. I also went through their pockets, took their money. We'd need all we could get until the presses started rolling.

I locked the back door, tossed the key into the bushes. If anybody wanted in they were going to have to break their way in. Somebody might do that the next morning, but with luck we had a month, maybe more.

Plenty of time.

I drove the Olds, backed it out of the driveway, hit the street and got going. I kept well under the speed limit, drove in the right lane, and got us the merry hell out of beautiful San Francisco. We both felt a hell of a lot better once we were on the open road, better still when we were across the state line.

We stopped at a place called the Golden d'Or Motel, a last-chance affair on the outskirts of a small Nevada town named Madison City. The name was fancier than the place itself. There were a string of a dozen tourist cabins, none of them painted since the owner bought the place, which must have been around the turn of the century. The owner's shack stood to one corner, a little larger than the cabins and, paradoxically, a little more run-down—maybe because it got more play. The VACANCY sign was permanently attached to the big sign announcing the name of the place. I don't think they had a NO VACANCY sign. I'm sure they never needed one.

I hit the brakes, killed the engine and tapped the horn. The owner came out, a long lanky man with a hawk nose and a pair of dusty blue jeans. He was wearing a ten-gallon hat and I guessed that he fancied himself a tourist attraction. He shuffled over to the car.

"Lucky for you," he said, "I got a cabin left." He had eleven like it, and they were also left but we didn't bother telling him this. Instead I signed the book—I think I used the name *Mr. and Mrs. Benjamin Harrison*—and paid the guy, and we piled out of the car and into the cabin. Luxurious it was not—old furniture scarred with cigarette butts and bottle rings, a creaking bed, walls that wouldn't stand up for a minute if a good wind ever blew across that section of Nevada.

We dropped into Madison City for a meal. There was one excuse for a restaurant in the town. I had eggs and coffee; Cindy had toast and tea. Neither of us was very hungry. Not for food.

So we left the excuse for a restaurant and returned to the excuse for a cabin, and we went into the cabin and locked the door behind us, and I turned to look at Cindy and she looked back at me and it began.

"We made it," she said. "We made it, Ted. We...did it, we finished it, we did the job. We're all set now, Ted. We're rich."

She was shaking like a leaf. This wasn't too hard to understand. All the pressures had piled up on her and she'd never fully cracked up. Now that we were safe, now that it was over, she was letting herself fall apart a little. I held her close and stroked her hair. It was unbelievably soft to the touch.

"It's okay," I said. "It's okay, baby."

"We did it. We did it, Ted."

"Easy, baby. Just relax, everything's all right, it's all over. Just relax."

She was shivering. "Suppose they find the bodies, Ted. Then what?"

"They won't find them for weeks."

Lawrence Block

"They might have found them already, Ted. You can never say for sure. Maybe somebody had to deliver a package to that house and decided something must be wrong."

"Why would they do that?"

She gave a little shrug. "I don't know," she said. "But it could happen. Or some nosy neighbor could decide something was wrong and call the police. You never know what's going to happen. I've read about cases that get solved that way. One slip of luck like that and the whole ballgame is over."

"It won't happen."

"But what if it did?"

I held her closer and rubbed the back of her neck. Deep down inside she wasn't as excited as she seemed. It was just the damned pressure.

"Listen," I said, "let's suppose the cops have already found the bodies. Personally, I think the odds against that are sky-high, but I'll concede the possibility. As you said, it could happen."

She didn't say anything.

"Even so," I went on, "we're about as safe as a government bond. They can't follow us. They don't know a thing about us, not a damned thing. As far as they're concerned, we're nameless and faceless. They don't know if there's one of us or ten of us. Nobody's looking for a man and a woman and nobody will."

"How about the car?"

"It's safe."

"Maybe somebody spotted it."

I shrugged. "It could happen," I said. "but don't stay up nights worrying about it. The car was clean when they drove up. It wasn't there very long before we were in it and out of the city. If it'll make you happy, we can get rid of it tomorrow."

"I think we should, Ted. There's no sense taking chances."

That was all right with me.

"And the money, Ted. The...counterfeit. That's another chance."

166

"It's no chance at all," I told her. "The bills will pass *banks,* for God's sake. And there's no way to tie up the job in San Francisco with counterfeiting. We got rid of all the junk in the place. Face it, baby — we're one hundred percent pure. Not even Ivory Soap can make that statement."

"I know, but — "

"But what?"

"But I'm scared."

She was scared — and she would go on being scared no matter how much talking I did. Her fear was emotional, not rational. It demanded an emotional solution rather than a profound logical argument.

Which was fine with me.

"Come here," I said.

She came to me and looked frightened.

"Me Tarzan," I said. "You Jane. That Bed."

She looked at me, at herself, and at the bed. A slow smile spread on her face. She understood completely and she was all in favor of the idea. But she stood there looking young and scared and virginal and left me to take good care of her.

While she stood there like a statue, motionless and beautiful and frightened, I took her in my arms and kissed her. Then I undressed her, taking her clothes off slowly but surely, my hands deft and clever. As each article of clothing left her person and became part of a crumpled heap on the cabin floor, more of her beauty was uncovered. It was like seeing her for the first time. I'd made love to her before — how many times? — but it seemed now that I had never realized quite how lovely she was.

It was uncanny. I had seen her on the street, then followed her only to discover she lived in the building right across from mine. And that little odd coincidence had led us to hell and back, from New York to Phoenix to Frisco to a broken down cabin on the outskirts of Madison City, Nevada.

And now we were going to make love again.

She stood stock still in bra and panties. I reached behind her, got my fingers on the hook of the bra. I took it off and saw the radiant beauty of her breasts. I wondered again why she bothered to wear a bra. She didn't need it.

Then the panties.

And then my goddess was nude. I took off my own clothes while she watched through sightless eyes. Then I picked her up in my arms without noticing her weight at all, and I carried her to the ramshackle bed, and I set her down on top of the sheet and stretched out beside her.

I kissed her. I kissed her mouth and her nose and her eyes. I stroked her cheek, her throat. I touched her breasts, felt the firmness of them, pinched the hard little nipples until they stiffened under my touch.

I ran a hand over her stomach. In time, when we were married, that stomach would swell up and blossom out with the weight of the child I would implant there. She would be pregnant with my son or daughter, and the two of us would have managed to create new life.

I touched all of her, her legs and thighs, her back, her shoulders. And throughout the process she remained entirely calm and completely motionless.

"I love you," I said.

And then it began. I took her once more in my arms, held her tight against me, and passion took over from fear. At once she came alive, alive for me, and I knew that everything was going to be all right. Her breasts cushioned me and her body made a place for me, and then it began in earnest.

It was a new kind of lovemaking for us. It was born in desperation, but it grew and developed with something not desperate or hectic at all. We were in love and nothing was going to stand in our way. We had it made — we were rich and free and nobody was chasing us.

Our lovemaking mirrored this. It was contained and yet unrestrained, passionate but gentle, complete but somehow calm.

There was no rush now, no need to hurry. For the first time in our relationship we were not pressed for time. Instead we had all our lives ahead of us, all the time in the world. And so we didn't rush. We took things easy, and we moved gently but firmly together, and I lay with the woman I loved and the world was now the best of all possible worlds.

She spoke my name and I spoke hers. She told me that she loved me and I told her it was mutual. But we did not talk very much because it was not very essential. Our bodies were telling each other everything that had to be said.

The bed strained under the weight of our love, its springs echoing the rhythms of passion. Outside, a wind was blowing up and it wouldn't carry the cabin away. I think if a wind had blown the cabin free from us we would have gone on doing just what we were doing. We'd never have noticed the difference.

Her body locked tight around me and our mouths merged in a kiss. It was going to happen now — our love was snowballing to a climax and no force on earth could have stopped it. The world was about to end — not with a whimper but with a bang.

And, at the crest of passion, she broke. She came to fulfillment with a rush of tears and a heave of sobs, and I knew that her fear and nervousness were over now that the crisis had been reached and surpassed.

Everything was going to be all right.

We slept well for the first time in a long time.

We found a dealer who wouldn't care about the fine points and traded dead-even for a cheaper car that was not in Reed's name. That gave us a clean car, which we traded again on a better model when we crossed another state line. If we had left any kind of trail it was covered.

We kept going. Heading east, leaving California as far behind as possible. The little tension that had remained with us was gone entirely when we hit Boston. Cindy was completely calm. I wasn't, not entirely, and I knew I wouldn't be as long as we had the plates and the press.

In a Boston hotel room I ran off two grand in twenties for spending money.

I opened a checking account in Rutland, Vermont.

I bought a weekly in Belfast, Vermont. Bought a house in Belfast, set up shop in the basement. Married Cindy, of course. That ought to go without saying.

Then I saved one-dollar bills.

And bleached them.

And turned them into twenties.

I printed a million dollars in twenties. Yes, a million dollars.

Then I got rid of the plates. I pounded them out of shape, tossed them into the hell box at the paper, made type out of them. It was better than throwing them in the river. I still own the press, however, and we use it for job printing at the Sentinel office. Handbills, stationery. Anything but money.

I make a damned good editor, the way it has worked out, and Cindy has developed into a damned good secretary. The paper needed money behind it to get out from under, and with the money I've poured into it, things are going pretty well.

Most of the million has been going into stocks and bonds, a little at a time. When it's all invested we'll probably leave Belfast, head somewhere else, some other town in some other part of the country. Buy a bigger paper, a bigger house, come in with more money and spend it without looking suspicious at all.

Sometimes we remember that very short period of time when we were hunters and hunted, criminals, murderers. Sometimes I remember Cindy putting a knife into Reed's back, killing him. She is pregnant now, and it is difficult to reconcile this lovely incipient mother with a murderess. Just as it is difficult to believe that I myself killed four men, one with a bullet in the throat, three more with a gun butt. I don't feel like a killer, or a criminal, or anything other than what I am—a small-town editor and publisher, a husband, an up-and-coming father.

A strange life. But a good one.

It's ironic, building a life of good from a life of sin and evil. It's not only ironic, it's impossible. Things like this just don't happen. Except maybe in fiction. But what's the old saw about truth sometimes being stranger than fiction?

Cindy and a hell of a lot of $20 bills kind of prove it.

I'm not complaining.

Afterword

by Lawrence Block

Look, this wasn't my idea.

Three or four years ago, Bill Schafer suggested that I might give some consideration to republishing a book of mine called *$20 Lust*, which had originally appeared as "by Andrew Shaw." I recalled the book he meant, but dimly; I had, after all, written it in 1960. But I didn't need to remember it all that vividly to know the answer to his suggestion.

No, I told him.

A little later I suggested he might want to publish a fancy edition of *Mona*, the first book under my own name; it had come out as a paperback original in 1961, and we could celebrate its fortieth anniversary with a nice limited edition hardcover.

Bill was lukewarm to the notion, but had an alternative proposal; how about issuing a double volume, containing *Mona* and *$20 Lust?* Once again, I didn't have to do a lot of soul-searching to come up with a response.

173

No, I told him.

Time passed. Then Ed Gorman, the Sage of Cedar Rapids, used an ancient private eye novelette of mine in a pulp anthology. When it came out he sent me a copy, and, while I didn't read my novelette—I figured it was enough that I wrote the damned thing—I did read his introduction, which I found to be thoughtful and incisive and generous. I e-mailed him and told him so, and he e-mailed me back and thanked me, adding that my early work was probably better than I thought.

"And," he added, "I really think you ought to consider letting Bill Schafer publish *$20 Lust*."

I felt as though I'd been sucker-punched. Where the hell did that come from?

So I got in touch with Bill. "I suppose I could at least read it," I said, "except I can't, because I don't have a copy." He did, or maybe he got one from Ed; in either case, a battered copy arrived in the mail. I looked at the first two pages, and I looked at the last two or three pages, and I heaved a sigh. Heaved it clear across the room, and would have heaved the book, too, but instead I hollered for my wife.

"Bill Schafer wants to reprint this," I said.

"Great," she said.

"Not necessarily," I said, and explained the circumstances. "I'd like you to read this," I said, "or as much of it as you can without gagging, and then tell me it's utter crap and I'd surely destroy what little reputation I have if I consent to its republication."

"Suppose I like it?"

"Not to worry," I said. "I'll sign the commitment papers, and I'll make sure they take real good care of you."

She found herself a comfortable chair and got to work.

While she's reading, I'll tell you what I remember about the book.

In the spring of 1960, I got married. My future ex-wife and I took an apartment on West 69th Street between Columbus and Amsterdam, and I installed a desk in our bedroom and planted a typewriter on top of it. I was writing a book a month for one publisher of what we'd now call soft-core porn, but which we then knew as sex novels. Veiled descriptions, no naughty words — but, within those limitations, as arousing as possible. Books, in short, to be read with one hand.

And I was doing other things as well, trying to write better books and stories for more respectable markets.

Sometimes a book would start out in one direction and wind up changing course. *Mona*, of which I spoke earlier, is a case in point. After I wrote the first chapter, it occurred to me that this might have possibilities. I stayed with it and wrote it as well as I could, and Henry Morrison, then my agent, agreed that it was a cut above the other stuff, and sent it to Gold Medal, where Knox Burger bought it.

Similarly, my second book started out as a TV tie-in novel, a $1000 quickie based on *Markham*, a short-lived detective series starring Ray Milland. I was pleased with the way it turned out, and so was Henry, and so was Knox; I changed the character's name from Roy Markham to Ed London, and called the book *Coward's Kiss*. (Gold Medal called it *Death Pulls a Doublecross*. In recent years its original title has been restored.)

Now where does *$20 Lust* fit into this scheme of things? Good question, and I'm not sure I can answer it. Ed Gorman sees it as a precursor to *Mona*, but I'm not sure that's the case; it may as easily have been written after *Mona*.

What I do know is that it represents a reversal of the earlier pattern, in which I'd started out to write a sow's ear and wound up with, well, call it a polyester handbag. I set out with the intention of writing a Gold Medal-type crime novel, and somewhere along the way I decided it wasn't good enough and finished it up as a sex novel. I don't remember when this happened, only that I was still at that desk and in that apartment at the time. (I was there for nine months, until the end of the year, when my ex-to-be and I moved to 444 Central Park West. We took the desk along, and indeed took it to Tonawanda, New

York, to Racine, Wisconsin, and to New Brunswick, New Jersey, where I had to cut two of its feet off in order to get it upstairs to my third-floor office at 16 Stratford Place. There, for all I know, it remains to this day.)

I called the book *Cinderella Sims*. My publisher called it *$20 Lust*.

And poor Lynne wound up stuck with the chore of reading it. Well, better she than I.

"It's not that bad," she said.

My heart sank.

"It's not," she said, just in case I hadn't heard her the first time. "It's not Shakespeare, but I don't think it'll do you any harm to publish it."

"Oh," I said.

"It's politically incorrect," she pointed out. "Sexist, racist, homophobic, at least in today's terms. But so's everything else written that long ago."

"Not to mention Shakespeare," I pointed out.

"Who mentioned Shakespeare?"

"You did."

"Oh," she said. "I did? I wonder why. Anyway, I think you should read it."

"Do I have to?"

She gave me a look, and she gave me the book, and I didn't exactly read it, because reading very early work of mine makes me sick to my stomach. But I skimmed enough of it to realize that it was a far cry from pornographic, and really didn't have much sexual content at all. I'd evidently gotten fairly far with it before I gave up on it and finished it for the sex novel house.

I wonder what made me do that.

Hell, who knows? Who knows why the kid that I was did any of the things he did?

What I had to decide was whether or not to republish the book. I weighed various considerations, and was reminded of Mae West's observation. When she had to chose one of two evils, she said, she made it a point to pick the one she hadn't tried yet.

Similarly, when I have to pick a course of action, I tend to choose the one that brings money into our house. And, while I don't suppose this very handsome edition of *$20 Lust* will wrap Lynne in sable, it should provide a few coins for that polyester handbag.

So there you are. It's a nice-looking book, isn't it? Well made, satisfying to hold in the hand. Even if you didn't get a lot of joy out of reading it — even if you never get around to reading it at all — I hope you take considerable delight in owning it.

Lawrence Block
Greenwich Village
December 2001

14